I Do Solemnly Swear

David P. McMullan

authorHOUSE®

AuthorHouse™
1663 Liberty Drive
Bloomington, IN 47403
www.authorhouse.com
Phone: 833-262-8899

Published by AuthorHouse 09/19/2024

ISBN: 979-8-8230-3316-9 (sc)
ISBN: 979-8-8230-3448-7 (hc)
ISBN: 979-8-8230-3317-6 (e)

Library of Congress Control Number: 2024918091

Print information available on the last page.

Contents

Contents

I Do Solemnly Swear

List of Characters

_____

The New Jersey Special Projects Task Force

_____

Jake Patrick - Director
Ava Matthews
Kent Baldauf
Tricia Highland
Gary Ceepo

New York City Anti-Terror Team

_____

Madeline (Maddy) Hampton - Director
Dennis McCollum
Mark Moorhead
Mary Ellen Tremblay
Billy MacDonald

Political Characters

_____

David James - Governor of the State of New Jersey
Phil Trooien (pronounced Troy-En) - New Jersey State Senator
Mrs. Roberta Trooien - Spouse
Howard Clarke - Chief of Staff for Senator Trooien
Liz Anderson - Aide to Senator Trooien

Daniel McGinnis - New Jersey Congressman
Deborah McGinnis - Spouse
Robert O'Reilly - Chief of Staff for Congressman McGinnis
Laurie Duffy - Aide to Congressman McGinnis
James O'Rourke - Speaker of the House

BAHRUN Terrorists

_____

Josef Habib
Abdul Farouk
Mohammed Sarif
Alaina Assis

Additional Characters

_____

Keri Ann Vernon Patrick - Jake Patrick's Spouse
Dakota Whalen - Lead Investigative Reporter for The New Jersey Herald
Bill Leininger - State Trooper working Security for Congressman McGinnis
Elizabeth (Lizzy) Warren - State Trooper working Security for Congressman McGinnis
Charlie Conroy - State Trooper working Security for Congressman McGinnis

About the Book

_____

"I Do Solemnly Swear" is a work of fiction.

I have used names of family and friends, as well as real places that do exist, to add credence to the storyline.

None of the events or persons depicted in the book have a basis in reality. All events and references to anyone real or imagined is purely coincidental.

I hope that everyone, whose name I have used for a character, enjoys the fictional part they play in this story and take their inclusion in high regard, as it was intended.

David P. McMullan

Dedication

I Do Solemnly Swear is dedicated to a principle that is close to my heart; patriotism.

As a child who grew up just a few years removed from the conclusion of World War II, I always took patriotism for granted.

Today, I'm not sure that the younger generations understand its importance.

Somewhere along the way, love of country, and all it stands for, has managed to become secondary to everyone's needs, wants and desires. We have forgotten our past and, in doing so, lost the meaning behind all those who sacrificed everything for the freedoms that makes America the greatest nation on the planet.

Too many people today place themselves above all else. Doing so places America in a vulnerable position, one that leaves us exposed to outside forces that do not have our best interests at heart.

Our greatest generation understood the need to place patriotism above all else, especially when threatened by those that wish to do us harm. Tens of thousands of our finest men and women placed themselves in danger to protect America and it's values, many of whom never returned to enjoy the fruits of their sacrifice.

It's the duty of every American to instill patriotism back into the hearts of our youth. Someday, they may be called upon to protect our freedoms once again. If they do not value what it is they are called to protect, I'm afraid they may no longer have the will to do what is required.

Everyone old enough to understand the value of patriotism must become educators to those that have come after them. Our schools may have dropped the ball on history, but knowing the past is the only way we can better understand the present and prepare for the future.

We must be a nation of patriots if we are to thrive.

David P. McMullan

Chapter One

And So It Begins

Wednesday, May 8th
Toms River Centennial Park
Toms River, NJ - 12:51PM

The New Jersey weather today could not be more glorious. With temperatures in the mid seventies and the sky as blue as the ocean, it is not surprising that supporters of the Congressman are packing the park in record numbers.

Congressman Daniel McGinnis is just minutes away from another rally. This is the first time he is holding one outdoors, allowing many more people to attend the event. It appears that he has accomplished his objective. The crowd is enormous and boisterous, just the way he likes it.

It's been three months since he announced his campaign to become the next Senator for the state of New Jersey. Since that fateful day, he has slowly climbed up the ladder of popularity, but still remains 10 points behind his incumbent opponent, Senator Phil Trooien (pronounced Troy-En), who has served in the Senate for the past 12 years.

To describe the Congressman as determined, focused and driven would not be hyperbole. His reputation in Congress is that of a bulldog, someone who will not back down on any issue that he deems to be important.

Having served just 4 years in Congress as the representative for the Middletown area, he has gone from a position of obscurity to being one of the more recognized politicians in the state.

There does not appear to be a TV camera or a microphone that he does not like, especially if he sees an opportunity to highlight one of his strengths or one of his opponent's weaknesses.

Dan McGinnis's primary issue on the campaign trail centers on the need for a stronger presence by law enforcement, as crime and security have been key sources of concern among the citizens of New Jersey.

While Senator Trooien has expressed similar concerns, the results have been less than satisfactory.

With the influx of illegals making their way throughout the continental United States, and the failure of the justice department to successfully prosecute crime in a manner that satisfies the masses, criminals have been less concerned with the potential consequences for their actions than they are with the actions themselves.

With six months to go before the election, the Congressman is presently focused on a number of recent terror related attacks across the country. Though small in size with limited success, these attacks continue to shine a light on the number of people in the country that should not be here. It appears that the majority of those captured were non-citizens, adding to the fear of a porous border and its impact on society.

It's been a long established campaign tactic, when running for office for the first time, to blame the present office holder for problems that are occurring under their watch. Congressman McGinnis is not an exception to that rule. Crime is up in the state and Senator Trooien is in power. Connecting the dots can be easy to do.

It's the prestigious senator, one of just 50 in the country, that can find it hard to hide behind the cloak of obscurity, something the Congressman is more than willing to point out. After all, what can a lowly Congressman, one among hundreds, accomplish compared to the elite of the Senate, or so the rhetoric on the campaign goes.

Today there appears to be a few thousand people in the park waiting for McGinnis to make his appearance.

With the music blaring and his staff preparing the crowd for his arrival, things could not be going better for the Congressman, who needs to find a way to make a dent in the Senator's lead.

Wednesday, May 8th
Office of the NJ Special Projects Task Force
Morristown, NJ - 1:05PM

As the task force prepares to leave for a presentation at Rutgers University, they are watching Congressman Dan McGinnis's political rally on TV.

Congressman McGinnis has just taken the stage to the roar of the crowd. It's obvious that he has garnered significant support over the past few months and Senator Trooien must be feeling the pressure.

3

As for the New Jersey Special Projects Task Force, they consist of 5 trained professionals whose job it is to keep the residents of New Jersey safe from terror threats within its border. To date, their success rate is one of the highest in the country and their accomplishments have not gone unnoticed.

Their director, Jake Patrick, is a former Navy Seal who has led the task force since its inception. His leadership skills and uncanny instinct has been a godsend for the state.

A few years back, his task force, along with the New York City anti-terror unit, prevented a major attack in the metropolitan area that could have killed hundreds, if not thousands. As a result, Jake was presented with the Medal of Freedom from the president, the highest honor a civilian can achieve.

While the task force may be small in number their impact has been enormous.

Their limited size is intentional, not a result of circumstance. Just as Navy Seal teams are small in number, for greater flexibility and secrecy, anti-terror units across the country need to be just as compact and resourceful.

Today, with numerous channels on the air 24 hours a day, the media is constantly competing with each other for anything newsworthy or even remotely of public interest. The last thing Jake's team needs is publicity. The larger the force, the greater the chance of exposure and the less likely they can remain in the background.

With the media constantly looking over their shoulder, Jake and his team cannot afford to have their activities monitored and dissected by others. Political correctness is a luxury they cannot afford.

The less the public knows about what goes into keeping them safe the better. While profiling may be a philosophical issue for some, especially those who, in an ideal world, believe both the oppressors and the oppressed deserve equal treatment, the task force needs to do whatever is necessary to protect Americans.

A successful mission requires preventing terror attacks before they occur. Any failure to do so can result in loss of life. Whatever methods are necessary to prevent such an attack is fair game.

Placing someone inside a mosque, for example, might be the only chance they have to expose a potential plot, if that mosque is thought to be compromised. It does little good to feign morality after lives are lost because of a failure to do everything possible to avoid the losses in the first place.

The Anti-Terror Task Forces throughout the country are among the elite the country has to offer. Their actions have saved thousands of lives over the past few years, even if no one knew of the danger and what steps were being taken to remove the threat.

As for Jake's team of professionals, they are the best of the best.

Kent Baldauf is a former member of Jake Patrick's Navy Seal team. He's a trained sniper and close combat specialist with an instinct for danger and the skill set to prevent just about any attack. His patriotism and love of country is unwavering. No one questions his dedication to the team.

Tricia Highland is a former Marine and a trained linguist, whose previous job was as a diplomatic interpreter for the United Nations. Her undercover work for the team, and her ability to blend into the background when necessary, has saved hundreds of people from disaster.

Gary Ceepo is a former Army Ranger and a capable combat specialist in his own right, who has the added responsibility of running interference between the team and the media. Being a former intelligence communications officer, he knows how to keep the press happy while telling them absolutely nothing of substance.

Ava Matthews is Jake's second in command, and a former Newark detective, who is the only team member with no military experience. When she was assigned to his team a few years back during a difficult case, her exemplary performance led Jake to ask her to become a member of his team, following the death of one of their own.

All four team members, as well as Jake Patrick, interact without hierarchy and with the understanding that all opinions and suggestions matter equally. Jake's management style would allow for nothing less.

As the team organizes their thoughts before heading out, some are not too happy about this upcoming assignment.

It appears that Jake's wife, Keri Ann, has managed to twist her husband's arm in an effort to get the team to provide insight to a class of future criminologist at the University. This is a graduate class that she is teaching and one that is about ready to leave the nest, so to speak.

Being a first rate profiler, who has assisted Jake and his team on numerous occasions over the years, this is his way of paying her back.

Jake, addressing his team over this unexpected assignment: "I'm sorry about this but as you all know, Keri Ann can be very persuasive."

Kent: "No kidding. What I don't understand is why we are all going? I'm sure they would be more than happy to see Jake Patrick standing in front of them. I feel like we are the E STREET BAND, backing up Bruce Springsteen, without the instruments."

Ava: "Kent, is there anything you prefer doing? Luckily, we are between cases at the moment and you, of all people, hate having nothing to do."

Gary: "I suggest you leave him alone, Ava. The last thing we need is having him in a bad mood in front of the class. After all, he's a walking lethal weapon."

Kent: "I can't tell you how funny all of your are. All I'm saying is this does not require everyone. After all, Jake is married to her, not us."

Tricia: "Kent, why don't you call Keri Ann and tell her that? I'm sure she will understand, allowing you to stay behind and do whatever it is you want to do. All the times she has helped us without reservation has to mean something? If you decide to make that call, please let me listen in so that I can hear your diplomatic skills at work."

Kent: "All right, I give in. Can't a guy express his opinion without being bombarded with criticism?"

Jake: "Okay, we had our fun. It's just an hour of our time and Keri Ann will be appreciative of our efforts."

As they are preparing to leave with the TV on in the background, Gary comments on the Congressman's remarks: "I really like that guy McGinnis. Anyone who is looking to beef up our police, while shining a light on the constant threat of terrorism, is okay in my book."

Jake: "I happen to agree with you. While I consider Phil to be a friend, he's got a real battle heading his way this November. Dan McGinnis is not going to fade away anytime soon."

Gary: "He appears to be the darling of the media as well. While that might not last, today he's the flavor of the month."

Jake: "Okay, let's get going. Everyone is going to participate in this lecture, not just me. I want Gary to start us off and pretend these students are the media. Get them interested without giving away any secrets."

Gary: "This should be a piece of cake, boss."

As the team heads out, their uneventful day will not end that way.

Wednesday, May 8th
Toms River Centennial Park
Toms River, NJ - 1:18PM

––––––––––––––––––––

Congressman McGinnis has everyone leaning in and listening to his every word.

This may be his most successful rally to date. Getting this many people out in the middle of the day should convince his

8

opponent that the Congressman is going to be a formidable threat to his reelection bid.

McGinnis: "For too long, Washington has provided the American people with lip service rather than action when it comes to protecting its citizens. While I know Senator Trooien does not favor open borders nor does he speak of cutting back our police presence, his words are of no value if they fail to garner the necessary action required to get the job done."

McGinnis: "I fear that Senator Trooien has become complacent, which is no place for anyone to reside who wants to change our country for the better. It's actions that matter. Anyone can mouth the words we all want to hear but the crime in our cities, and the danger from terrorists that might be living among us right now, can no longer be satiated with words."

As he continues to excite the crowd, his security staff find themselves overlooking a mass of humanity that is moving closer to the podium. There are no seats in the park for the attendees so everyone is standing.

As Dan's rhetoric continues to raise the temperature and the patriotic zeal of those in attendance, they begin moving closer to the stage, ignoring the barrier fence that serves as a buffer.

One Week Earlier

The Governor of the state for New Jersey, David James, has called Congressman Daniel McGinnis to the capital for a meeting.

As his popularity continues to grow and the crowds become larger, the governor fears that his exposure needs more than just his campaign advisors watching his back. After exchanging pleasantries and the normal introductory banter, they get down to business.

Governor James: "Dan, I'm going to call an audible, if that is okay with you? I'm going to assign a few security guards to your campaign for the duration. The crowds are growing larger and the publicity you are garnering does not just attract your supporters, as I'm sure you are aware."

McGinnis: "Do you really think that's necessary, Governor? I haven't seen anything to suggest that I'm in any danger. The last thing I want to do is to place a firewall between me and my supporters. My message is one of unity and common interests. I want everyone to consider me one of them, not one of the ruling class that keeps their distance from the masses."

Governor James: "While I understand your concerns, you are a representative of our state and I've seen less vulnerable situations result in tragedy. This is not a request on my part. They will stay in the background as much as possible but they will be there just the same."

As the Congressman slumps his shoulders slightly, aware that his argument is falling on deaf ears, he pushes on: "How many guards are you considering?"

Governor James: "There will be three in total. Two will be assigned to be within a few feet of you at all times when you are out among the voters. The third will remain anonymous and work the crowd, searching for anyone or anything that might appear suspicious."

Governor James: "For the most part, I suggest you forget they are there. Let them become second nature and just do your thing."

McGinnis: "I understand. When do you suggest we implement this new security protocol?"

Governor James: "There's no time like the present. Let me introduce you to your new security team."

With that said, three officers are led into the governor's office, two male and one female. They are all dressed in casual clothes that might be worn at a sporting event rather than a political rally. The surprised look on the face of the Congressman says it all.

Governor James: "No one said they had to look like members of the Secret Service."

As they both laugh a little, the three agents smile and embrace their latest assignment by shaking hands and ignoring formality. None of this banter negates the seriousness of the situation. They are assigned to protect the Congressman and keep him from harm for the remainder of the campaign.

Back to the rally on May 8th

The three security guards assigned to the Congressman's detail are all veteran State Troopers. Bill Leininger has been on the force for 15 years, Charlie Conroy has been a trooper for 9 years and Elizabeth Warren (no relation) has been on duty for the past 6 years.

The team has designated Lizzy, which is what her friends call her, to be the one working the crowd. While Bill and Charlie stay near by, Lizzie's job has been made more difficult by the amount of shoving going on as many of the those in attendance try to get closer to the Congressman.

Dan McGinnis's last remarks about the need to keep America safe has led the crowd to begin chanting "USA" over and over again, forcing him to remain silent until the chants fade away into the distance.

As the crowd continues their boisterous chants, Lizzie notices a man in a hoodie that is quietly on the move. He appears to be making his way closer to the platform, moving through the noisy supporters with a purpose that does not mirror the rest of the crowd.

Lizzie, over her coms: "Guys, there's a man in a green hoodie at 12 o'clock that is moving closer to you. I'm not sure what is going on but he needs to be carefully watched. I sense he's not a typical supporter."

Charlie's the first to spot him: "I got him. He's making his way closer but I do not see him making any attempt to disrupt as of yet. I won't take my eyes off him until I'm sure he's no threat."

Bill notices him as well and he decides not to take any chances. He steps down from the platform, placing himself directly in front of the Congressman and at eye level with the suspect that is still twenty feet away.

As the guy in the hoodie continues weaving through the crowd, he gets within 12 feet of the platform, just one person away from Bill. Without warning, he reaches into his pocket, seconds before being tackled by Bill and dragged to the ground.

As the crowd looks on, startled and confused, a shot rings out from nowhere and strikes Charlie Conroy in his left shoulder, throwing him to the ground at the foot of the Congressman, who decides to drop to the floor, trying to avoid a follow-up shot from the unknown shooter.

The crowd is now aware of the attack and everyone starts running in all directions, trying to get away from the danger that has invaded the rally.

As chaos ensues, those in charge remain focused on the matter at hand.

As the Congressman's aide dials 911, Lizzie heads directly to Charlie to provide assistance while Bill smashes his suspect's face into the ground, securing his hands behind his back with cuffs.

As he pulls the man in the green hoodie to his feet and reaches into his pocket, the only thing he can find is a cellphone. The frightened man appears to be in shock and all he can say is: "All I wanted was a picture for my wife. She loves the Congressman. What did I do wrong?"

As Lizzie reaches Charlie, he waves her away: "Get the congressman out of here."

After Bill searches the man carefully, he realizes he's no threat and sends him into the arms of one of the local police officers to be held for further action. He them turns his attention back to Charlie, who is in a great deal of pain. As he tries to lift him to his feet, the pain emanating from his shoulder is too great to permit that to happen.

Luckily he can hear the ambulance approaching in the distance. With the crowd dispersing and the park looking more like an open field again, the last thing they need is to remain out in the open, allowing the shooter another chance to finish the job.

As Lizzie gets McGinnis into his car, she orders him to lie on the floor and away from the windows. She then exits the car and heads for her partners in the park. The ambulance arrives on the scene seconds later, with the EMT's sprinting with the gurney toward the wounded officer.

It's obvious to all three that the shooter is no longer out there. They turn their attention toward Charlie who is being administered the necessary pain killers that will make it easier to move him. His shoulder blade appears to be completely shattered, the ramifications of which will require extensive rehab.

No matter how prepared you are for the worst, no one expects this to happen during a political rally in the park. The real work must now begin in earnest. They must find the shooter before any more casualties begin to accrue.

Chapter Two

The Fog that is War and Politics

Wednesday, May 8th
Senate Office of Phil Trooien
Washington, D.C. - 1:46PM

Senator Phil Trooien, along with his Chief of Staff, Howard Clarke, are in a heated discussion with one of Phil's fellow colleagues over the upcoming appropriations bill.

As the dialogue continues there's a knock on the door. Without waiting for a response, his campaign aide calls out to him as she enters: "I need to talk to you right away sir. Something just occurred that you need to be aware of."

Trooien: "It's okay, please come in Liz. What's so important?"

As Liz Anderson enters, the expression on her face tells a story within itself: "There's been a shooting at the McGinnis rally in Toms River. A security guard was seriously hurt. I suggest you turn on your TV."

As the Senator reaches for the TV remote, his chief of staff, Howard Clarke, can sense that whatever happened will not be good: "Based on Liz's expression, I surmise that this will not be helpful for our campaign."

As Phil turns on the TV, he sees a reporter at the scene anxiously trying to describe what has just occurred.

Reporter: "I can't describe how chaotic the scene is here in Toms River. As the rally was under way, one of the Congressman's security detail left the stage to confront a man in the crowd. Almost at that exact moment, a shot rang out from nowhere, striking Charles Conroy, another of the Congressman's security team, in the shoulder, dropping him to the ground. He was standing directly in front of the Congressman at the time of the shot. I suspect Congressman McGinnis was the intended target."

Liz Anderson: "Every channel is covering the shooting. All of the major networks had reporters there covering the rally. It took less than a minute for the stations to begin broadcasting the rampage."

Trooien: "Did they capture the shooter?"

Liz: "As best I can tell, they have no idea who fired the shot or where they were shooting from at the time. It's too early to figure much of anything out."

Trooien: "What about the man they confronted in the crowd?"

Liz: "It looks like he was just a fan trying to get a close up picture of the Congressman. I'm sure they will look into every detail but he appears to be innocent."

Trooien: "I can't believe this. In broad daylight someone tries to take him out. What the hell have we come to in this country?

We better get a handle on things quickly or we will no longer have a country at all."

The Senator turns toward his colleague, letting him know that the meeting in over. As his fellow senator leaves the office, Phil begins changing channels to see for himself the wall to wall coverage that is taking place.

After listening to a number of the reporters on different networks, it is becoming apparent that no one knows anything of substance other than the obvious. Someone took a shot at the Congressman, missing him but striking one of his security guards. No matter how they try to create additional details, that's all there is to know for the time being.

As Phil turns off the TV, he addresses Howard with a concerned look on his face: "This is bad, Howie. If there is still anyone out there that does not know Dan McGinnis or his campaign against me for the Senate, they do now."

Clarke: "If we get out a statement right away, we can turn this into a positive. Your stance on crime has been called into question by McGinnis on a number of occasions. Let's beat him to the punch and send a strong message before Dan has the time to try and spin this his way."

Trooien: "Don't you think that any remarks that even hints at politics right now could backfire?"

Clarke: "Not if we choose our words carefully. If we allow him to control the narrative, the public will sympathize with him and we will start losing ground in the poles overnight. We must take the high road and empathize with Dan on this. Give the public two candidates who are strong on crime, not just the one who was targeted."

Trooien: "The sympathy vote alone could bring him closer to me in the poles. While I'm glad he's okay, we need to rethink our overall strategy."

Trooien: "Whatever we do must walk a fine line between concern and outrage. If we don't get the attention turned back in our direction, someone else may be sitting in my seat come November."

Trooien: "We can't properly express outrage from Washington. Its best that I do it from home. We'll leave tonight for Bedminster."

Wednesday, May 8th
Office of the Governor
Trenton, NJ - 1:54PM

With the TV running in the background, Governor David James is on the phone with the state trooper, Lizzy Warren: "Lizzy, I need to know every detail of what has transpired from you, not the media. First of all, is Dan okay?"

Lizzy: "The Congressman is shook up, for obvious reasons, but he is okay. I'm more concerned right now about Charlie. His shoulder is in bad shape. The bullet did a lot of damage. Bill and I are doing everything we can to protect the Congressman."

Lizzy: "We are driving on the parkway right now heading back to his campaign office. I asked the Congressman to remain on the floor and away from the windows. Can you arrange for a police detail to meet us there?"

Governor James: "That won't be a problem. I'll have them there within the next half hour. Right now I need you to bring me up to date on what happened."

Lizzy: "Having such a large crowd with no seating made our job a lot harder. Everyone was loud and aggressive, but in a good way. They were cheering and smiling but there was a lot of pushing, especially among those who wanted to get closer to the podium."

Lizzy: "Making my way through the crowd was difficult but not impossible. I first spotted a man wearing a green hoodie who appeared to be out of step with the rest of the crowd. He was slowly and methodically making his way closer to the stage, looking less like a supporter and more like a man with a purpose."

Lizzy: "I alerted Bill and Charlie to his presence and expressed my concerns. Bill immediately spotted him and jumped down from the platform to block his path to the Congressman. Charlie remained on stage and placed himself directly in line with the suspect, blocking his view of the Congressman."

Lizzy: "I continued to scan the crowd for any other potential suspects. When I saw nothing, I began heading toward the man in the hoodie from the rear, boxing him in between Bill and myself."

Lizzy: "All of a sudden, I saw him reach into his pocket and before I could react, Bill had him on the ground, immobilizing him in the process. It was at that moment that the shot rang out and Charlie was hit, forcing him to the ground. The rest was a blur. Chaos ensued and the place resembled a stampede of bodies."

Lizzy: "All the guy had in his pocket was a phone which he claimed was going to be used to get a closeup photo of the Congressman for his wife. We will look into him closer but my gut tells me he's a dead end."

Governor James: "I can't think of another case that is more important for us to solve at this time. Taking a shot at a Congressman during a rally tells me that he has ticked off the wrong people. While I know that the political climate can get pretty nasty, this is on another level entirely."

Lizzy: "Once the police arrive at the Congressman's office, Bill and I would like to head over to the hospital, if that is okay with you, Governor?"

Governor James: "I understand. I hope Charlie will be okay. Call me from there and fill me in on his condition. Right now, I'm going to have to light a fire under the Toms River police department. They need to place every available officer out there looking for the shooter."

Wednesday, May 8th
5 miles from Rutger's University
New Brunswick, NJ - 2:04PM

As Jake and his team are getting closer to their destination, his phone rings in the car. With the phone linked via bluetooth to the car's communication system, everyone inside can see that the call is coming from their office in Morristown.

Jake, answering the call: "This is Jake Patrick."

Jake's Administrative Assistant Ann is on the other end: "Jake, I thought it was important enough to contact you. There has been a shooting at the McGinnis rally in Toms River. Someone appears to have taken a shot at the Congressman, hitting one of his security guards instead. It's all over the news."

Jake: "How badly was he hit?"

Ann: "It appears to have struck his shoulder blade. No one has any further details."

Kent, speaking from the back seat of the car: "I hope he had enough security with him to get him the hell out of there. Where is he now?"

Ann: "I have no idea but based on the news reports, he was whisked away quickly and is no longer in the area."

Gary: "This is going to be a media nightmare for the governor. The longer it takes to get to the bottom of this, the more the press will hound him for answers."

Jake: "I'm sure Governor James is doing everything he can. We have some top notch investigators in the state and I suspect he will be making calls to all of them about now."

Ava: "Maybe you should call him, Jake. It wouldn't hurt for you to offer our services, if need be? We rarely have downtime but this happens to be one of them."

Jake, turning his attention back to his assistant: "Thanks for letting us know, Ann. Keep in touch if anything major develops." He then disconnects the call.

Tricia: "It's not such a terrible idea to offer our help. If this was a potential terror attack, we would be his first call."

Jake: "The last thing I want to do is to step on the toes of those who will be assigned to this case. Politics plays a part in every department. What does it say about the expertise of our crime investigators if we overstep our directive and begin intruding on their domain? The governor does not need that extra pressure. If he sees a need for our services, I suspect he will be the one calling."

Gary: "I have to go along with Jake on this. The media would have a field day questioning our involvement. As for the local investigators, their competence would be called into question, which could lead to a number of problems for everyone."

Jake: "Let's put our energy into today's seminar. That's the only assignment we have at the moment and I doubt anything is going to change in the next few hours. Keri Ann deserves our best and that is what she's going to get."

Forty Two Minutes Earlier

Wednesday, May 8th
621 West St. - Apt 2B
Toms River, NJ - 1:22PM

_____

As the political rally is in high gear, Josef Habib, a key member of BAHRUN, one of the more radical international terror organizations, is taking in the rally from behind his rifle scope. He has an important job to do today and he is looking forward to carrying out his assignment to the letter.

BAHRUN has a special place in their black hearts for both the United States and the New Jersey Special Projects Task Force. On a number of occasions, they have made significant threats to our homeland only to have their attempts thwarted by none other than Jake Patrick and his team.

Though the Task Force remains high on BAHRUN'S hit list, today is another matter. Josef's assignment is simple, direct and to the point.

As he tries to drown out the chants of USA coming from the crowd, he lines up his target and prepares to turn the rally from a political event into a chaotic gathering where no one feels safe or secure.

As Habib prepares to take the shot, his thoughts turn to initiating the plan that's about to be put into motion. Once he pulls the trigger, there will be no turning back.

As he focuses on his assignment, he begins slowing his breathing to ensure he locks onto his target. Once everything is in place, he squeezes the trigger.

As he sees his target fall to the ground, he can hear the screams beginning to drown out the chants. Within seconds of firing, he is on the move, heading as far away from the park as possible.

The first salvo is now launched and things are going to get a lot more interesting as the days go by.

BAHRUN'S latest war on America is just getting started.

Back to the present

Wednesday, May 8th
Centennial Park
Toms River, NJ - 3:15PM

_____

In the aftermath of the shooting, the newly designated crime scene is becoming overcrowded with police personnel from a number of surrounding jurisdictions.

Because of the notoriety of the case, the governor has ordered multiple departments to put their best people on this, knowing all too well that the press will be watching their every move.

The complications facing the investigators are enormous.

There's no way of determining who actually was in attendance. The notification of the event was sent to tens of thousands of potential supporters along with a number of media ads promoting the event.

There were no invitations, no guest lists, no check-in stations or attendance monitors. Anyone wanting to hear the Congressman were let in, adding to the anonymous crowd that became witnesses to the attempt on the life of a candidate for Senate.

While they did arrange for everyone to pass through a metal detector before entering the park, this was not the most ideal venue to maintain control.

The actual fencing surrounding the park was not designed to protect people from entering the park. It could easily be scaled or circumvented, if a person had a mind to do so, including a few of the natural tree barriers located throughout the park grounds.

To make matters worse, the attendees disappeared in the chaos of the moment, hoping to avoid becoming targets of a madman. If the shooter hid among them, he picked the safest environment to hide in plain sight.

All the investigators could do is hope that anyone with viable information would come forward to provide assistance. Until that happens, they would spend their time analyzing the crime scene and the surrounding buildings for any clues as to what transpired.

A team of forensic analysts were gathered in the media van looking over all of the press footage at the rally. Some of the them were broadcasting before the Congressman arrived on the stage, provided an opportunity to observe a number of the attendees that were in the background of their broadcasts. With no information of value as of yet, no one could be excluded from the suspect's list.

On the plus side, most of the press had video of the actual shooting, though some of the cameras moved off the stage following the security guard that was confronting the man in the green hoodie.

As for the investigators on the grounds, they are in need of a miracle, hoping to stumble on to a clue that would lead them in the right direction, rather than the organized chaos that appears to be the order of the day right now.

The first good news came from the forensic technicians.

After examining a number of different videos that captured the actual shooting, the analysts all agreed that the shot came from beyond the park. It originated from the Northeast corner and traveled at a trajectory that would have the shooter somewhere between 12 and 16 feet above ground level.

The most promising location appears to be about a tenth of a mile from the stage with three buildings situated within the proper angle parameters. Two of the buildings are three story apartments while the third is a single story food market with a flat roof.

If the analysis is correct, the shooter could have been either on the roof of the market or in one of the second floor apartments facing the park. They now had a direction to pursue and they wasted no time heading toward the buildings in question.

The sudden movement of those in charge toward the far end of the park did not go unnoticed by the press. As a number of them tried to follow behind, the local officers refused to allow them to pass, leaving them agitated, quickly expressing their displeasure.

One of those reporters, a late arrival to the scene, remains away from the others, choosing to concentrate her efforts on finding a way to get around security. She has not made it to the top of her field by letting others dictate her movements. Successful reporters need to be their own investigators, something her readers have come to expect from her.

As the other reporters pressed against the newly created barrier, imploring the officers to let them get through, Dakota Whalen was nowhere to be found, as she headed in the opposite direction. She decided to circumvent the block and arrive at her destination from the other side.

Dakota Whalen is a successful investigative reporter for the New Jersey Herald, one of the leading publications in the state. Her unorthodox style and fearless nature has led to a number of scoops that has left many of her competitors in the dust.

Dakota was just another struggling reporter a few years back when she caught the attention of Jake Patrick during a major terror related case. She managed to provide

the task force with some critical information and that led to her gaining Jake's trust, providing her with a valuable friend in high places.

Since that fateful day, Dakota has married her long time boyfriend Chris and she has lost none of her fervor or any of her resolve when it comes to getting a story.

Who knows, if she's lucky, she may be able to talk her way into one of the buildings that could be ground zero for this attack. Following the rules have never been high on her list of priorities. Today would be no different.

Chapter Three

_____

Circling the Wagons

Wednesday, May 8th
Congressman McGinnis's Campaign Office
Middletown, NJ - 3:23PM

_____

The congressman is still trying to recover from the shock of today's events.

While he remains in his office, there are two detectives in the outer room waiting to talk to him. Under different circumstances, they would not have allowed their subject this much leeway but they have decided to wait patiently, at least for the time being.

Robert O'Reilly, Dan's Chief of Staff, is inside with him trying to calm him down before he meets with the authorities: "I know this was bad but you have to get a grip before talking to the cops."

O'Reilly: "You cannot afford to come off as a person not in control of his emotions. Anything you say or do might get back to the press. You need to be sympathetic concerning Charlie and his injuries while remaining steadfast in your convictions."

McGinnis: "Steadfast in my convictions? What the hell does that mean? I was the target of a shooter that barely missed taking me out. A few inches in the other direction and it would be me in the hospital or the morgue for that matter."

O'Reilly: "I know it could have been worse but it did not turn out that way. You are gaining in the poles because you have a strong and unapologetic message. We cannot allow anyone to see you emotionally impacted by the attack. This is the perfect time for you to become more defiant, not less."

As they continue to discuss how best to handle this failed attempt on the Congressman's life, someone is knocking loudly at the office door: "Dan, its Debbie, please let me in. I have to see that you are all right. Open the door, please."

Deborah McGinnis is Dan's wife, who must be worried sick, as she arrives at his office in a state of shock. Nothing will appease her other than seeing for herself that her husband is unharmed and in one piece. She learned of the attack from TV news, which was not the best way for her to hear that her husband was the target of an assassination.

The Congressman is well aware that he failed to call his wife immediately after the attack. His nerves were so shot that all he could think about was putting as many miles as possible between himself and the shooter.

Things have not been great between them these past few months. Debbie was just getting used to the attention the family was receiving from Dan's appointment to Congress. She's a great deal more private than he is and was not on board when he decided to run for the Senate, which would only make the attention more intense.

His failure to make that phone call after the shooting will not lower the temperature one bit. They are gradually growing apart and this could only make matters worse.

As O'Reilly opens the door, Debbie storms into the room, carrying a complex mixture of emotions that range from relief to anger. While her sense of relief is reinforced, as she sees her husband sitting at his desk as if this was a normal Wednesday, the anger she feels, being left out of the loop, is in full view.

Debbie, running over to Dan: "I don't see any blood so the report that you were unharmed appears to be correct. As for you lack of concern for me, that's another matter."

As her anger builds, she turns toward Robert: "I can understand why Dan might not have been in a state of mind to call me right away but I should have been your first call. Learning about this from a TV reporter is unacceptable."

Dan: "It's not Bob that's to blame for my stupidity. No matter the trauma of the moment, I should have realized the power of the media and put you at ease before the reports hit the air. All I can say Deb is that I'm sorry."

Debbie: "Where do we go from here? If there is a madman out there trying to kill you, how can you really be protected until he is found and put behind bars?"

O'Reilly, trying to lower the temperature: "I'm sure this is an isolated incident. Someone crazy enough to take a shot in broad daylight will not be hard to find."

Debbie, turning to her husband's Chief of Staff: "And you know this how?"

Dan "Let's take this down a notch, please. Going forward, all rallies will have to take place in more secure venues. Doing one outside in a park was a lapse in judgement on our part. We have to be more careful in the future."

Debbie: "You know my feelings about this entire campaign. When you decided to run and chose crime and terrorism at the center of your campaign, you opened yourself to pushback from the worst society has to offer."

Debbie: "If you decide to continue this campaign as recklessly as you have to this point, you will be doing so alone. Neither myself or the boys will make any public appearances nor will we answer any questions from the press at all. You might as well be single in the eyes of your constituents."

O'Reilly: "Are you aware how much that could hurt Dan in the campaign? The last thing we need is the press wondering about the stability of his marriage as he runs for the Senate. Anything that takes their focus off his campaign will damage his chances."

Debbie: "If you think that will get me to back off you're mistaken. I was not on board with this campaign from the beginning. The only way I will play along is if I'm given a seat at the table, beginning right now."

Debbie "While my involvement can remain in the background, as far as the public is concerned, this campaign will not make any decisions that are not agreed upon by all three of us. If that's a problem, then we revert to plan A, which leaves Dan without a supportive wife and family."

Debbie: "I must be part of every decision being made and my voice must carry enough weight to influence those decisions. We do this as a team or I'm out, the consequences be damned."

As all three remain silent, Debbie glares at both of them, looking for their decision. As they quietly nod their heads in agreement, she sits down in the chair across from Dan's desk: "Okay, how are we going to handle the police officers waiting outside?"

Wednesday, May 8th
621 West St.
Toms River, NJ - 4:09PM

―――――――――――――――――――――

After examining the roof of the food market, finding nothing to suggest that it was the location of the shooter, the investigators are preparing to enter one of the two apartment buildings adjacent to the store.

What they failed to notice was the arrival of Dakota Whalen, who was able to enter 621 West Street carrying a bag of groceries, pretending to be one of the residents. Her calm demeanor and expression of concern for all of the commotion, was a performance worthy of an Oscar. None of the officers in the street even considered the possibility that she was not who she pretended to be, allowing her to enter the building unaccompanied.

As she enters the building, Dakota figures that she has no more than ten minutes to begin knocking on doors, hoping to get an interview with someone who may have seen the shooter.

The building has six apartments, two on each floor of the three story building. As she starts with the bottom two apartments, she gets no responses. Finding no one home in the middle of the afternoon on a weekday, is not all that unusual.

As she makes her way to the second floor, an older woman opens her front door and runs directly into Dakota in the corridor: "I'm so sorry miss, you startled me. I just wanted to see what all of the fuss is about out front. Are you one of the officers looking around?"

Dakota may push the envelope of credibility but she avoids outright lies. As she nods, which might assume agreement, she responds: "I'm investigating the shooting that occurred at the political rally outside in the park. Are you aware that a shooting occurred?"

Tenant: "I had the TV on but I was in the kitchen and missed all the fuss. By the time I realized what had happened and got back to the TV, the crowd was running in every direction. I was afraid to open the door until I saw your people out front."

Dakota: "There's a good chance that the shooter might have been in your apartment building. Did you see anything that might help? Anything that might be out of the ordinary?"

Tenant: "I did hear someone knocking on my neighbor's door awhile back, which is somewhat unusual. Millie lives alone as do I, and she rarely leaves the house. The only visitors I ever see her with would be on the weekends when her family sometimes visits. I was going to knock on her door myself before running into you. She has a better view of the park."

Dakota: "I suggest you go back inside for now. Let me talk to Millie. If she saw anything, I'll let her know of your interest and she can tell you directly."

As the tenant re-enters her apartment, Dakota crosses the corridor and begins knocking on Millie's door. Receiving no response, Dakota decides to accompany her knocks with a verbal request: "Millie, please open up. I just have a few questions about

the shooting that took place in the park. I'm asking everyone in the area if they saw anything that might help in solving this. You are not in any trouble so please open the door?"

As Millie fails to answer, Dakota's senses are beginning to gnaw at her. According to the neighbor, Millie rarely leaves the house and she apparently had a visitor a short time ago, making it less likely that she would not be home.

As she tries to deal with a rush of anxiety over what may be behind the door, Dakota notices that the investigators are heading into the building. She had hoped to knock on the doors of all six apartments but that seems highly unlikely right now.

Making matters worse, she knows the head investigator, having interviewed him on a number of occasions. The ploy she used on the beat cop to get into the building will not get her out. Sometimes all you can do is ask forgiveness rather than permission, especially when its too late for the latter.

Carrying her grocery bag, she begins her trek from the second to the first floor. The head investigator recognizes her immediately as he stops by the staircase, waiting for her to reach the bottom: "Could Dakota Whalen actually reside in this building? I suspect your commute each morning to your office in Hackensack would be a long one."

Dakota: "I'm just doing my job detective. I guess intelligent minds think alike. I suspected that this apartment building might be ground zero for the shooter so I thought I would look into it."

Detective: "How did you get in here? You do know that lying to an officer could result in you being placed into custody?"

Dakota: "I never lie to anybody. I just carried my paper bag up the stairs and into the building. I can't help it if your people thought that I lived here? That error in judgement is not on me."

Detective: "What's in the bag?"

As if on cue, Dakota opens the bag and removes her pocketbook, crumpling the bag in the process. With a sly smile, she tries to leave the building only to be blocked by a handful of officers.

The detective responds: "Before you go, I suggest you tell me what you may have learned while in here. While you may not have lied to an officer, holding back critical information from me can result in you being charged with obstruction of justice."

Dakota: "Unfortunately, I learned very little. I only made it to the second floor with three of the apartments apparently empty. The only person I was able to interact with resides in apartment 2A. She does not appear to know anything at all, though she would love to talk to you, especially if you can enlighten her as to what went on. Being a busy body is not a crime, at least not yet."

Detective: "Since you told me that you do not lie, are you telling me that you learned nothing of importance?"

Dakota: "I wouldn't say nothing. There is a sliver of information that may or may not help you that I'm willing to share, if you promise to truthfully answer a question for me?"

Detective: "I'm not too keen on sharing, especially at the start of an important investigation. If what you know can help us to move forward, I suggest you reconsider your hesitation."

Dakota: "It's more a feeling than it is a revelation but I have been known to be quite intuitive. Why not listen to my question before you decide not to answer?"

The detective ponders how best to react before he responds: "I guess hearing your question does not require me to accept your terms, so ask away."

Dakota: "What did you learn about the attack that led you to descend on this location with your entire investigative team?"

As the detective contemplates his response, he decides that providing her with the details would only allow her a few hours of exclusivity, thus worth the risk: "Our tech experts determined that the shot originated someplace higher off the ground than one could achieve from the park. These three buildings fit the profile and are located in the right trajectory to be the potential hiding place of the shooter."

Dakota: "So the shooter had to be someplace in this vicinity. Because of the height of the trajectory, I have to assume the first floor apartments are no higher than the park so the shot had to come from either the upper floors or the roof of the market."

Detective: "Based on the trajectory, the third floor apartments and the apartment roofs would be too high off the ground, so we are concentrating our efforts on the second floor apartments as well as the roof of the single story market next store."

Dakota's mind is now operating in overdrive. Since the investigative team had already searched the market roof before heading inside the apartment building, the market must not have proven to be fruitful. Her information may be more valuable than she thought. She might be a resourceful journalist but she would never intentionally impede an investigation.

It's now apparent to her that Millie's apartment could be ground zero. She turns to the detective before responding: "An older woman by the name of Millie lives in Apartment 2B. She should be home right now but no one answered when I knocked. To make matters more confusing, her neighbor in 2A swears she heard a person knocking on her door just before the attack in the park. If I'm correct, that could very well have been the shooter."

Detective: "Are you sure that this Millie is still in her apartment?"

Dakota: "Of course I'm not sure of anything. There's no way she did not hear me knocking on her door and calling out to her. If she is still inside, she may not be able to get to the door or she may be prevented from doing so. All I know is she did not come to the door."

Detective: "Maybe she was afraid to answer the door? Some older people are fearful of strangers. Not responding to you might be her way of protecting herself."

Dakota: "Her front window faces the park. When you arrived outside you did not do so quietly. One look out her window would tell her the authorities were going to be entering her building. She would have answered the door if she was able to do so."

Detective: "Okay, I see your point. I suggest you head out and leave the detective work to us. I will concentrate on Apartment 2B. What we find out will be in our public report at some time in the near future and then you can read about it along with everyone else."

As Dakota heads out of the building, a sense of dread overcomes her, sending shivers throughout her body. What if someone did answer the door and it wasn't Millie? She may have dodged a bullet today. In fact, it might be time for her to re-think her aggressive behavior when looking into a story.

As she heads to her car, she realizes that once this feeling subsides, who she is as a journalist is more important than being just another reporter who does their investigating over the phone.

As long as she remains at the top of her field, risk will always be in play. She knows no other way of doing her job.

Wednesday, May 8th
Josef Habib's Vehicle
Somewhere in New Jersey - 4:41PM

As Habib is heading to a very important meeting with his fellow loyalists, he is feeling calm and confident, after having completed the first task of many that will lead to the demise of Jake Patrick.

As he continues to replay the events of the past few hours in his head, his phone rings. He can see that the call shows on his screen as being from an unknown caller. While that could mean that the call is just another bothersome spam call, his instincts tell him something else.

As he prepares himself, he answers the call with a friendly hello.

Unknown Caller: "What the hell happened, you were not supposed to hit anyone?"

Habib: "As I was pulling the trigger, the security guard quickly moved in the direction of my warning shot. These things happen. On the plus side, it was not a lethal wound. I'm sure he will be okay."

Unknown Caller: "We just started this fear campaign and we already have a glitch. I'm not paying you for mistakes. If you want the rest of your money you will make sure that there are no more mishaps."

Habib: "Everything's going to be okay. Besides, the wounded guard will insure that they take this attempt seriously. A missed shot might lead the authorities to believe it came from some crazy who is out of control."

Habib: "The plan was to put them on notice and to have them preparing for the possibility of further attacks. The guard lying in the hospital ensures us they will take this seriously. I see it as a Win-Win."

Unknown Caller: "I will let you know when you need to take the next step. I hope you avoided leaving any clues that will have the authorities at your door. That's a problem we both cannot afford to have."

Habib: "There's no need to worry. They will find nothing of value to help them. They will just be spinning their wheels until the next attack. Besides, the longer this remains on the media's radar, the better."

Unknown Caller: "I'm taking a big chance here. I was told that you are the best and that I could trust you. Don't make me doubt our arrangement."

As the call ends, Habib smiles to himself. This unexpected arrangement has allowed himself and his fellow jihadists a chance to accelerate their plans to finish the job that others were unable to do.

This time will be different. Jake Patrick will not see this coming and he will pay the ultimate price for his past actions that have left BAHRUN licking its wounds. It will be the task force that will be mourning their leader when this is finally over. I Do Solemnly Swear

Chapter Four

A Jihadist in Our Midst

Wednesday, May 8th
621 West Street - Apt 2B
Toms River, NJ - 5:03PM

After their discussion with Dakota Whalen, the investigators wasted little time breaking into Millie's apartment, only to find her lying dead in the corner of the interior hallway. The search for the location of the shooter is over.

As they begin a detailed search of the apartment, the first step is always the accumulation of fingerprints. This is a laborious task as there are hundreds throughout the apartment.

When taking numerous fingerprints from the scene, most, if not all, could easily be those of the tenant.

As to what might be of immediate help, they recovered a cigarette butt from the window sill in the living room that overlooks the park. While there does not appear to be any usable prints, it is a strange brand that is not readily available in the states. A portion of the remaining butt has some writing on it that suggests it is Turkish, not American.

David P. McMullan

Another useful clue is an ejected cartridge shell found inside the hem of the window curtain. It must have discharged from the rifle after firing, landing in a spot that the shooter could not locate in time before leaving the apartment.

On further examination, the cartridge came from a Winchester 300 Magnum, a mainstay for snipers during the Iraqi War. The Arctic Warfare Magnum, a lightweight sniper rifle from the United Kingdom, appears to be the most likely weapon.

Due to the lethal nature of the bullet, the security officer's shoulder wound must be extensive. It appears the shooter did not intend to have the Congressman walk away from this in one piece.

Whatever the motive behind the shooting, having two viable clues to the identity of the shooter gives them a direction to pursue. Its time to contact their superiors with an update. Thankfully, the call will not be without substance.

Wednesday, May 8th
418 Fairfield Road, Apt 3A
Fairfield, NJ - 5:22PM

_____

Inside Josef Habib's apartment, a meeting is in progress.

There are four people in attendance, all of whom are part of a dormant cell of BAHRUN loyalists planted in the Northeast, waiting to get their chance at creating chaos on American soil.

In addition to Habib, there is Abdul Farouk, Mohammed Sarif and Alaina Assis.

Abdul owns a muslim religious store in Paterson, NJ. The community has a large Islamic population, providing him with significant cover as he hides his radical affiliation in plain sight.

Mohammed Sarif is a truck driver for a local delivery service who spends most of his day driving between north and central New Jersey. He manages his own hours, giving him a great deal of leeway, as long as he completes his deliveries for the day.

Alaina Assis, the only female member of the terror cell, manages a local fitness center. Her job is to oversee the center for a corporate conglomerate that owns the facility, one of many in their portfolio.

Having a number of trainers under her wing allows her a signifiant amount of freedom, if the need to be away from the center arises.

As for Josef Habib, being the oldest among them, he is well financed by BAHRUN, allowing him to play the part of a retired successful businessman.

He was sent to America 4 years ago to put together a loyal team of jihadists, which could be called upon, at any time, for assignment. Today, that assignment has been identified. They are to eliminate Jake Patrick, who has been a thorn in the side of BAHRUN for the past few years.

As the meeting continues, Habib is bringing everyone up to date on his day: "Things are proceeding perfectly. I suspect the authorities have found the right apartment by now and are in possession of the clues I left behind. If my plan works as expected, we will get our wish shortly."

Mohammed: "Why did you decide to injure someone rather than just scare the Congressman, as was the request of our benefactor?"

Josef: "The more I thought about it, the more I was concerned that a missed shot could be interpreted as being the work of an isolated psychopath. I needed them to suspect an assassination attempt by terrorists."

Alaina: "While I can understand your concerns, that's not what our benefactor wanted you to do. Might you have jeopardized our relationship?"

Josef: "I've already communicated with the benefactor. We are good to go. The first step is getting Jake Patrick assigned to the case. The clues I left behind should accomplish that part of the plan."

Josef: "As for now, I suggest you all return to your lives as if nothing has happened. I will be in touch when necessary."

Wednesday, May 8th
Jake Patrick's Home
Morristown, NJ - 6:21PM

As Keri Ann, Jake's wife, is preparing dinner, Jake is in the living room watching ESPN.

During the rare moments when he has some down time, Jake turns to his second love, baseball and his beloved METS, a team that requires a great deal of patience from their fans.

They are presently enjoying a three game winning streak, which is a bit of a rarity. Its days like this when the fans begin to believe that this year might be the year they finally become champions, something they have not done since 1986.

Keri Ann: "Jake, dinner will be ready in a few minutes. Why don't you wash up before I start plating the food?"

Jake: "I need just a few more minutes. Sports Center is about to show the highlights of last night's win."

Keri Ann: "Is that two wins in a row?"

Jake: "This is their third win on a row. I'm hoping this starts a trend that will get us closer to the playoffs."

Keri Ann: "You say that every time they win more than one game. I think your father owes you an apology. If he was a Yankee fan, you would have enjoyed a life with less suffering."

Jake: "My dad started out as a Brooklyn Dodger fan. Anyone who supported the Dodgers could never like the Yankees. That would be against the laws of nature."

KeriAnn: "If you don't wash up, your food will get cold. I'm putting it on the table right now."

As Jake and Keri Ann are having dinner, she decides to comment on his presentation today to her class of graduate students: "I really appreciated you making the time for me and my class. I could tell, by the level of concentration, that they were listening to every word."

Jake: "I was happy to do it. You have helped us on numerous occasions and the least we could do was return the favor."

Keri Ann: "I got a little nervous when, during the Q&A, one of my students asked Kent about his experiences in the field. As

45

we both know, Kent's ability to filter his responses leave a lot to be desired, but I must say, he rose to the occasion."

Jake, smiling as he recalled the moment: "I felt the same way about it. Kent tried to get out of coming today but the rest of the team reminded him of your past assistance. I think they embarrassed him into coming along, which did not guarantee that he would behave himself."

Keri Ann: "Well, he surprised us both, and for that, I was extremely grateful. I told him so after the class. He just shrugged his shoulders and acted as if it was just a normal day for him. Showing emotion is not one of Kent's strong points."

As they were finishing their dinner, Jake's phone rang as he looked over to Keri Ann before answering it. As she gave him a nod of approval, he went into the living room to retrieve it.

Jake: "Its Governor James calling, I'm going to have to take this."

Jake: "Governor, I'm surprised to hear from you at this late hour?"

Governor James: "I'm sorry to bother you at home but I had to reach out to you. There's a chance that the shooting today in Toms River might be connected to terrorism. There were a few pieces of evidence to suggest as much, thus the reason for my call."

Governor James: "When someone takes a shot at one of our politicians, it guarantees national exposure, which places it high on our list of priorities."

46

Jake: "I understand your concern. Such a bold attempt in broad daylight suggests to me that those responsible are not going to run away and hide."

Governor James: "My thoughts as well. Why don't we meet at your office tomorrow morning at ten? Because of the clues left behind, I'm assigning your team to handle this investigation, no matter how to plays out."

Jake: "Our team welcomes the opportunity to help."

Governor James: "Okay, I'll see you tomorrow."

As Jake ends the call, ho looks over at Keri Ann with a look of both concern and determination: "The attempt today on Dan McGinnis's life is showing signs of being terror related. It's now our case to solve."

Keri Ann: "This already has national attention. I doubt you will be able to keep things under wraps on this one."

Jake: "I know it's not ideal but we are going to have to live with it.

Keri Ann: "As always, if I can be of any help, all you have to do is ask."

Jake silently mouths the words THANK YOU as he begins the process of contacting his team about their new assignment. Any downtime they were hoping to have will have to wait.

Wednesday, May 8th
Home of Senator Philip Trooien
Bedminster, NJ - 7:36PM

―――――――――――――――――――

As Phil and Roberta Trooien try to relax in the living room, it's becoming apparent that their efforts are not working.

Roberta: "I can't imagine how terrifying it must have been to come within inches of losing your life. Dan must be having seconds thoughts about continuing his campaign."

Phil: "I doubt that thought entered his mind. If public opinion has any value, I suspect he's waiting to see if the polls begin to show their concern for his safety in the numbers."

Roberta: "The hell with public opinion, if you ask me. Someone tried to kill him. If I'm a member of his family, nothing else matters."

Phil: "The last poll had him ten points behind. I suspect he's a lot closer today than yesterday. If he plays his cards right, he can capitalize with the voters, making this race a lot tighter. That what I would do, if things were reversed."

Roberta: "You can't be serious. Having your life threatened to obtain political office is nothing short of insanity. I'm sure the Debbie is telling Dan the same thing right now."

Phil: "Well, I can't wait around to see what happens next. I'm now on the defensive and what action I take immediately could have a significant impact on my political career."

Phil: "Howie and I have arranged for a morning press conference that will give us an edge with the voters and limit the impact Dan might receive from the shooting. Anything to move the needle back in my direction."

Wednesday, May 8th
Home of Congressman Dan McGinnis
Sparta, NJ - 7:56PM

Now that Dan'e family is gathered together at home, Debbie is trying to get things back to normal, which appears to be a losing battle.

Talking to their two sons, trying to prepare them for school tomorrow, where their classmates might be bombarding them with questions, has already blown a hole a mile wide in their plans. The expressions on their son's faces tell it all; their father nearly died.

Dan considered having them stay home from school but Debbie would have none of that. All that would accomplish would be to forestall the inevitable. The quicker they address matters and show a desire to return to normal, the better.

With the boys upstairs in their rooms, Dan expresses how he feels about the events of the day: "I'm trying hard to dispel my anxiety, but I'm not winning that battle. If I'm unable to shake this fear, I don't see how the public will not notice my emotional state?"

Debbie: "I'm sure this will pass. Until you feel better, we just have to limit our exposure as best we can."

Dan: "I'm glad you are part of the team. Having you on board will go a long way in helping me alleviate the anxiety."

Debbie: "We are in this together."

Just then, Dan's phone rings, causing him to jump a little, startled by the unexpected call: "Who the hell is that at this late hour? Can't everyone leave us alone?"

Debbie can see that the call is coming from the Speaker of the House, Jim O'Rourke: Jim's on the phone, you have to take his call. Take a deep breath and keep your emotions in check. He must hear a confident and determined voice on the line."

As Dan prepares for the call, he hits the talk button: "Hey Jim, how are you doing?"

O'Rourke: "I'm calling to check on you, not me. I thought you might call me earlier but when I did not hear from you, I decided to check in. I can't imagine how you must feel."

Dan: "After the initial shock wore off, my determination to continue with my campaign has been stronger than ever. We can't allow the crazies to get away with this type of intimidation. If we let them win, no politician will ever be safe."

O'Rourke: "That's a noble thought but reality can be a hard pill to swallow. Having someone shoot in your direction is a lot more serious than empty threats or implied actions that tend to remain unfulfilled. Don't make the mistake of treating this with less concern than it deserves."

Dan: "I can't deny how frightened I was at the time. It's what you do next that matters. I'm committed to continuing my campaign to be the next sitting Senator in the state of New Jersey."

O'Rourke: "I'm going to put an amendment on the floor by the end of the week to condemn all forms of violence toward sitting house members and I will be looking for the vote to be unanimous."

O'Rourke: "If you are up to it, I want you to speak on behalf of the motion in front of Congress. It will go a long way to uniting the House when it needs it the most."

Dan: "Of course, just let me know when you need me to attend."

O'Rourke: "I appreciate your desire to help. If there is anything you need, you just have to ask."

As the call ends, Dan takes a big sigh of relief as he tries to regain his composure: "I felt like an actor playing a role. I hope I was convincing."

Debbie: "I'm proud of you, Dan. That was perfect. As for the race, I suspect that the next poll will indicate that we are closing the gap. Adversity can work in both directions."

As the couple silently try and relax, they both understand that the long, uphill road to the Senate has just gotten started.

Chapter Five

Assigned to the Case

Thursday, May 9th
Office of the NJ Special Projects Task Force
Morristown, NJ - 10:16AM

It's a rare day that the Governor shows up at the task force office.

Fortunately, the team had a heads up from Jake beforehand but it still has everyone a little nervous and a bit on edge. The normal banter is missing today. Everyone is on their best behavior and the formality of it all has Jake a little out of sorts.

Jake: "Before I have the governor fill us in, I expect this meeting to be like any other held here in the office. Everyone's opinions are welcome and encouraged. The Governor wants you to hear from him directly as to why this case is being assigned to us. I expect all of you to be direct and forthright with your questions."

Governor James: "We have been fortunate to have you looking out for us these past few years. Your efforts on our behalf has saved hundreds of lives and no one has more respect for what you do than I do."

Governor James: "I want this to be an informal meeting. You can refer to me as Governor, or David, if you like. Today I'm just another member of the team. The last thing I want is for you to hold back your opinions because I'm in the room."

Ava smiles in his direction before responding: "That's easier said than done, governor."

Kent chimes in: "As everyone here knows, I'm the least formal member of this team. With that said, there is no way I'm calling you David. I guess governor will have to do."

As everyone laughs at Kent's remarks, they all nod their heads in agreement. The meeting can now begin in earnest.

Governor James: "Yesterday's shooting has garnered national attention. It's been a long time since a politician found themselves in the crosshairs of an assassin's bullet."

Governor James: "The reason I'm here today has to do with two pieces of information collected at the scene of the attack suggesting the possibility of this being terror related."

Governor James: "The first clue was a Turkish cigarette butt while the second was the discharged shell from the sniper rifle. It was a Winchester 300 Magnum shell, which our ballistic experts believe came, most likely, from a bolt action rifle manufactured in the United Kingdom."

Kent: "This is not the first time we have come across this ammo. The most likely weapon would be the Arctic Warfare Magnum rifle, a staple in the middle east. Its use among local terror cells during the Afghanistan War explains the possible ties to terrorism."

The Governor nods in agreement as he passes out photos of both the shell and the cigarette butt to the team.

As everyone examines the photos, Tricia Highland is the first to speak: "I recognize the cigarette. It is definitely Turkish and a brand that would be difficult to find in the states, if at all. I doubt that anyone living in America would be smoking this brand. Most smokers could not function without their daily nicotine fix. Choosing a brand that is hard to come by makes little sense."

Governor James: "The cigarette butt was sitting in the corner of the window sill in the living room, where we feel the shooter was positioned at the time. As for the shell, it had fallen into the hem of the window curtain, making it invisible to the naked eye, until it was removed. The investigators felt that the shooter could not readily retrieve it and did not want to waste any more time at the scene looking for it."

Kent: "Everything about this screams amateur."

Gary: "I agree with Kent, nobody who is looking to get away with murder would leave a cigarette butt behind in plain sight."

Ava: "As for the shot itself, only an amateur could miss so badly from that distance. Why an amateur would have such a high powered weapon is a question that needs to be answered. An amateur would use an easily obtained hunting rifle with a scope, not a sniper rifle."

Governor James: "Speaking about the shot itself, we were fortunate to have dozens of videos of the shooting from the media in attendance. After studying all of them, we

came away with the one view that captured best the moment of impact. I sent that link to Jake this morning."

As the Governor was speaking, Jake was hooking up the large screen in the conference room to his lap top. As everyone focused on the screen, the video began running. It had been edited to begin about a minute before the shot was fired and to run for a minute after the bullet struck Officer Conroy.

As it begins, Congressman McGinnis is talking to a large number of his supporters. To his left is one of his security guards, Officer Charlie Conroy, the person who was wounded in the attack. On his right is Officer Bill Leininger, another of his security team.

Maybe thirty-seconds before the attack, the camera catches Bill Leininger eyeing someone in the crowd before quickly jumping down from the platform. He then begins moving straight ahead and out of the range of the camera.

As if on cue, Charlie Conroy begins moving closer to the Congressman, in what appears to be an attempt to place himself between the person of interest and McGinnis.

Shortly after making his move, you can hear the shot ring out as Conroy is thrown to the ground by the force of the impact. Within seconds, the crowd reacts and the rally turns into chaos with people running and ducking everywhere.

As the Congressman appears to gain control of his emotions, he jumps down from the platform, landing close to officer Conroy, trying to remain close enough to the ground as if this might place him out of view of the shooter.

Just before the camera shot ends, Officers Lizzy Warren and Bill Leininger make their way to the Congressman, shielding both of them with their bodies until help can arrive.

As the video ends, everyone turns their attention back to the Governor, as he remarks: "The investigators believe that the sudden movement of both security guards, especially Conroy, led to the bullet missing its target, hitting him by mistake."

Kent: "If the guard blocked his shot, why was the shot taken? I'm sure that a better one was just around the corner. No one in the park was in fear of being targeted. All the shooter had to do was wait a few seconds and McGinnis would be in the morgue right now."

Governor: "I would think this further established that the shooter was an amateur, someone acting on emotion."

As Jake's team ignores the governor's response, they begin to interact among themselves. Governor James can sense that they are better left on their own. As he rises from his seat, preparing to leave: "Jake, your team can take it from here. Just remember that I'm here to help if you need anything."

After the Governor says his informal goodbyes, he leaves the office.

Jake: "I know that having the governor here was a bit restrictive. No matter how many times someone tries to put you at ease, it's still the governor."

Ava: "Well, we are alone now and we have an important case to solve. I suggest we get all of our opinions on the table."

Tricia begins the discussion: "None of this makes any sense. No one leaves such an obvious clue as a foreign cigarette butt at the scene. As for the shell casing, it would never end up in the hem of the curtain. Shells discharge with a fair amount of velocity, sending it farther away from the window, not straight down toward the floor."

Kent: "To take this one step further, I believe the entire scene was a setup, which tells me that they wanted us to believe that its terror related. The question is why?"

Gary: "The obvious answer is that they wanted us to head down a rabbit hole that would take us farther away from the truth."

Jake: "Gary's right, they wanted us to believe this was a terror attack. The real question is why?"

Tricia: "Whether the clues left behind were intentional or not, it was because they pointed toward terrorism that we were put in charge of this investigation. Who would benefit from having us running the show?"

Jake: "Let's put that on the back burner for a moment. I think we all agree that the clues left behind at the scene appear to be intentional. The shooter was not a loose cannon out to make a point. This was all planned in advance."

Kent: "Then why isn't Congressman McGinnis dead?"

Ava: "We can't explain it on face value. Something may have distracted him at the moment the shot was fired. Maybe someone knocked on the door? Maybe there was some unexpected activity in the street below the window? There had to be something that caused the shot to go awry?"

Kent: "I'm not buying it. The only reason he's still alive is because the shooter never intended to kill him in the first place. The plan was to scare him, not kill him."

Gary: "If everything went according to plan, who would benefit from having frightened the Congressman to such a degree?"

Ava: "What about someone on Senator Trooien's staff that might have thought their day in the sun would be over if Trooien loses the election?"

Tricia: "If the plan was to miss, it's not a stretch to believe that someone in the McGinnis camp might try and get him some added traction from an attempted assassination. He's still far enough behind in the polls to benefit from the sympathy vote."

Kent: "So what exactly are we saying, Jake? I'm more confused now than when we started. We have to decide on a course of action or we won't get anywhere. Terror? Crime? Political Intrigue? What direction do we go in?"

Jake: "I'm starting to believe that the terror connection might be real, though not the primary reason behind the attack. What if the person responsible hired someone to take the shot? If that person had ties to terrorism, they might have decided to use this event to kick off their own agenda."

Gary: "And what agenda might that be?"

Jake: "Why is our team handling the shooting?"

Tricia: "I see where Jake is going. We are only involved because the clues left behind hinted at a possible terror connection. What if the shooter wanted us to be the team doing the investigation?"

Kent: "Plant the terror clues and they will come."

Jake: "Tricia, can you check into your network of contacts to see if you can find out anything that may be relevant? Let's not tell anyone about our suspicions regarding the shooting until we are able to fill in a few of the missing pieces."

Jake: "We need to begin by interviewing everyone that has a connection to McGinnis, especially his opponent. We can start arranging those interviews right away. Finding the person behind the attack is the fastest route to the shooter.

As the team begins to put an action plan together, they, once again, find themselves facing a potential terror threat, one that might have political ramifications.

Politics can be a brutal game but it's rarely lethal. Whoever put this into motion might have taken on more than they can handle.

Thursday, May 9th
Josef Habib's Residence
Fairfield, NJ - 11:48AM

_____

Josef Habib smiles as he receives a text from the benefactor.

Jake Patrick and the NJ Special Projects Task Force has been put in charge of the investigation. Jake Patrick plans on interviewing everyone connected to the Congressman, starting this afternoon.

Its time for Habib to prepare a proper welcome for Mr. Patrick, one that will come as a complete surprise to him. For now, Habib needs to keep the benefactor happy, at least until he can place Jake Patrick in his crosshairs.

Chapter Six

It's Always About Politics

Thursday, May 9th
Offices of The New Jersey Herald
Hackensack, NJ - 11:54AM

The paper has been celebrating all morning. They got the jump on the rest of the media following the shooting inToms River.

The Herald was the only news organization, including the networks, to have pinpointed the location of the shooter at the time of the attempt on the life of Congressman McGinnis.

Dakota Whalen, who has been a star reporter by all conventional standards, was the first to report such critical information. Her contribution to inform the public cannot be understated.

By all accounts, the Herald's online newspaper has more than doubled their hits for a single day and they have seen their number of registered newcomers increase by nearly 5%, which is a new record for one day subscriptions.

As for Dakota, the early edition is over and its time to work on her next story, yet to be written. There is more to do and she wants to be the first to let the public know what is going on behind the scenes of the investigation. Her standards are higher than most, but that's her goal every time she puts pen to paper, to quote a phrase.

The news that Jake Patrick and his team are being put in charge of the investigation might have come as a surprise to many of her colleagues but not to her. Jake's team is the best and this case requires nothing less.

When she was a rookie reporter, trying to earn her wings, she managed to get on the good side of Jake by not reporting critical information she obtained about one of the terror plots that he was investigating.

Jake showed his appreciation for her loyalty with an exclusive interview after the plot was foiled and the public was safe from harm. That interview put her on the map, a position she has maintained and nurtured to this day.

With Jake Patrick in charge of this investigation, she needs to find a way to, once again, place herself in a position that can benefit both of them. After all, you can't ask for a favor without providing one in return. That's why many of her fellow journalist fail to achieve their objective. They expect cooperation to be a one way street.

Dakota knows that she can contact Jake and he will take her call. Her instincts tell her that would be a mistake unless she can offer him something of value. **Quid Pro Quo** is more than just a saying.

As she contemplates her next move, she sees an opportunity to come in the back door, where no one appears to be looking. While her competitors seek out the prime players, such as

Congressman McGinnis or Senator Trooien, it might be more productive to start with someone near the inner circle but still close enough to be privy to facts and details that might provide the public with valuable insight.

A few years back, when Dan McGinnis was campaigning for office for the first time, Dakota was able to establish a rapport with Laurie Duffy, Dan's trusted aide. They hit it off right away, primarily because Dakota did not come off too aggressively. A few glasses of wine and a gentle nudge can go a long way.

Laurie, having known McGinnis for a number of years prior to the election, found it easy to talk about the man rather than the political figure. The resulting article, penned by Dakota, provided the public with a more personal understanding of who McGinnis was, which added a great deal of humanity to her reporting, something most journalists fail to capture.

Maybe Laurie can provide her with something of value that will help her along the way?

After all, who knows what you may learn, especially if you know what questions to ask.

As Dakota settles on a course of action, she makes the call that might just earn her a seat at the table, a seat right next to Jake Patrick himself. Hopefully Laurie is willing to have another glass of wine with an old friend.

Thursday, May 9th
Office of Congressman McGinnis
Middletown, NJ - 11:58AM

The Congressman's office is a bit chaotic this morning, which should come as no surprise after yesterday's shooting.

To make matters worse, the Congressman canceled his early morning staff meeting. He always starts each day with a pep talk and words of encouragement. Failing to do so has many of his supporters a little apprehensive.

To add to the confusion, it appears that Dan's wife Debbie has decided to take a more active role in his campaign, arriving with him this morning. Within a few minutes of their arrival, the door was closed as the two of them, along with the Chief of Staff, Robert O'Reilly, barricaded themselves inside.

While the campaign staff went about their day without the pep talk, the recent arrival of Jake Patrick and Ava Matthews added to their concern. Is everything okay? Is the campaign proceeding as planned? Hopefully, before the day ends, everything will be made clear.

With rumors running rampant, especially a report that terrorism might be responsible for the attack, it's hard for the staff to ignore the terror angle when Jake Patrick is on premises. A lone gunman with a grudge is one thing but a terror cell looking to create havoc is far more concerning to the staff.

As Laurie handles the Congressman's phones from her perch outside his office, she finds herself leaning in toward the door to try and hear the conversation that is just a few feet away, though all she can decipher is low muffled sounds that do not resemble anything remotely similar to English.

As she leans in closer to the door, she is startled by the phone. As Laurie tries to regain her composure, she answers the call: "Congressman McGinnis's Office. How can I help you?"

Dakota Whalen: "Laurie, this is Dakota. We haven't touched base in a while but after yesterday's shooting, I just had to reach out to you. You must be living a nightmare about now. How are you doing?"

Laurie: "I'm okay. It's the Congressman that has a lot to deal with, not me."

Laurie, sounding a little suspicious: "I'm assuming you are calling me to help fill in some of the details you can use in your next article. I've already heard from a number

of media outlets this morning, all looking for their next headline. We are not ready to discuss anything about the shooting. When Dan is ready to talk, I'm sure he will make the necessary statement to the press."

Dakota: "Laurie, you have this all wrong. I have plenty of sources to bother when it comes to the shooting. This call is personal. I'm just calling from one friend to another. There's no way you can get yourself back to normal this quickly without support. I was hoping we could meet for a glass of wine later today. I promise you that nothing about the shooting will be on the agenda. All I want to do is comfort a friend."

Laurie: "That's nice of you but I'm not sure I would be good company right now. It seems as if the campaign has gone off

64

course for the time being. Until Dan can right the ship, this is an office without a rudder."

Dakota: "That's another reason you need to take a step back. You're the only person standing between Dan and the masses right now. That can be an unbearable burden for one to carry. Let me give you a break from the chaos, even if it's only for a few minutes."

Laurie, thinking it over, as she looks out into the bullpen area at people pretending to be busy: "Okay, what the hell. I can meet you around 5:30, someplace between the office and my home, but I can only stay for one glass of wine. I need to get home early."

Dakota: "Great, I promise to make sure you don't stay out late. I'll meet you at McNulty's pub on Central at 5:30."

Laurie: "I'll see you there. Now I need to get back to work."

As Laurie hangs up the phone, she smiles to herself. She enjoys Dakota's company. It will be fun to see just how Dakota tries to wriggle something of value out of her while pretending to be talking about the weather. At least Laurie will be playing the game with someone she likes.

———————————————————————

Inside Dan's office, the conversation is proceeding with relatively few insights that might help Jake and Ava in the investigation.

The Congressman appears to be in the dark as to how he became a target. While he may be a candidate for the Senate, none of his opinions or platform issues are that controversial. The only thing that separates him from his opponent has more to do with Senator Trooien's implied failure to initiate significant changes, not a difference in philosophy.

When change fails to materialize, the one with less responsibility has the advantage, which is how Dan chooses to approach the key issues of crime and terrorism. Once I'm in office, things will finally get done.

Politics is a ruthless business. For every success, there is always someone out there to point out one's failures, even if those failures are based on perception rather than fact.

No one will ever say that politics is fair. It's a blood sport that few can survive, much less thrive. Whoever has the more credible rhetoric wins. The voters would not be happy to learn that, most of the time, they are just pawns in the game.

Politicians use distraction as an art form. Look toward the shiny object over here because there's nothing to see behind the curtain.

It doesn't matter whether you're the Wizard of Oz or just a Congressman looking to take the next step forward in his political career, everyone hides some of the truth behind a curtain that only a select few can see.

Jake: "Are you sure that there has not been some note, letter or phone call that has come into the campaign that may have given you or Bob pause? People rarely act out their frustration without having expressed it in a less than lethal way prior to an attack."

Bob O'Reilly, Dan's Chief of Staff, feels obligated to respond: "There are so many crazies out there that its hard to know what might be real and what is just white noise."

As this point, Debbie McGinnis decides to respond, reinforcing her position of importance in the campaign: "Of course we get a number of emails that attack Dan for a number of reasons."

Debbie: "We make judgement calls every day. Outright threats to his life or health would be passed on to the authorities. While I'm not aware of anything to date that has risen to that level, the process would be the same."

Bob O'Reilly: "I agree with Debbie, I'm not aware of anything of that nature. The hate mail we receive is about issues they disagree with, not threats of violence."

Dan: "Let's not forget the emotional mail from those that love Phil Trooien. How dare we run against him, or so it goes. I'm aware of nothing that might be a precursor to such a violent attack."

Ava: "Don't underestimate emotional ties. Love and hate are a lot closer than one might think."

Dan: "I understand, according to the governor, that there were clues at the scene that suggests the possibility of this being terror related. Is that true?"

Jake: "The jury is still out on that. Because terror remains on the table, my team has been asked to run point on the investigation, though nothing about this case suggests, with any certainty, such a connection."

Debbie: "What were the clues that led to your team being in charge of the investigation"?

Ava: "I'm afraid that information is confidential. The less details revealed, the better the chance we have of finding the shooter without tipping our hand."

Jake, turning his attention back to the Congressman: "Were you aware of anything out of the ordinary when the shot rang out?"

Dan: "Nothing that comes to mind. I was so into my speech that I must have blocked out everything else. I never saw the person in the crowd that my security guards were concerned about nor did I notice Bill Leininger leaving the stage, ready to confront him, if necessary. I did notice Charlie Conroy moving closer to me just before being struck but his movements were so slight that they never registered as a concern."

O'Reilly: "Well I guess we were all lucky that the shooter was such a bad shot."

Debbie: "When Dan suggested the outdoor rally, I tried to talk him out of it but I was not as forceful as I should have been. It's amazing how hindsight can be so clear after the fact."

Ava: "How close were you to Charlie Conroy?"

Dan: "We were not close at all. When the Governor insisted on providing me with security protection, we accepted all three of them into our fold. I found them to be easy to be around and pleasant enough but it was all business, nothing personal."

Debbie: "I find that to be an odd question. Do you think that Charlie was in on the attack?"

Jake: "That's not at all what we are saying. When someone is shot, we have to consider all possibilities. What if Charlie was the target, not Dan? Maybe something in his personal life led to the shooting. We are just covering all bases."

O'Reilly: "That seems to be a ridiculous notion, if you ask me. Taking a shot during a political rally in broad daylight because of a vendetta against one of the guards is a bit of a stretch."

Dan: "Unless the person is outright crazy, which would make him easy to find, the risk vs. reward is too great. I put myself at risk when I insisted on the outdoor rally. Charlie was wounded because of me. I must have been the target."

Debbie: "Dan is right, Charlie was wounded because he got in the way of the shot meant for Dan. We owe him a debt of gratitude, not suspicion."

Jake: "We've gotten off track. In our opinion, the rally proved the perfect opportunity for the shooter to either eliminate the Congressman from the campaign or to send a message that Dan needs to rethink his campaign all together. It's the second part that we need to consider."

O'Reilly: "Are you saying that the shooter intentionally missed?"

Ava: "It's a distinct possibility. From the shooter's perch across the street, it was not that difficult of a shot. Who would benefit from having Dan drop his campaign bid for the Senate or, at least, tamper his messaging?"

The Congressman was just beginning to alleviate his anxiety. The confusion he's experiencing over these alternative scenarios appears to have resurrected the emotional trauma that followed the attack.

Dan: "I'm feeling anxious from all of this speculation. It's bad enough having been shot at by a distraught zealot with limited skill. The possibility that a pro might have been involved that could have killed me in an instant but chose not to, it far more disconcerting."

Debbie: "Oh my God, if what you say is true, Dan is not out of the woods. Where do we go from here? To bow out of this campaign would be the same as committing political suicide."

Jake: "Let's take a breath for a moment. Who benefits the most from Dan dropping out of the campaign?"

Debbie: "It would have to be Senator Trooien. We have been slowly gaining on him over the past few months and who knows what someone might do when they see their political career heading out the door?"

Dan: "There's no way I can believe that Phil is behind this attack. We may be adversaries at the moment but he's the last person I see taking such drastic measures."

Dan: "Besides, he still leads by 10 points. That's a huge lead in politics. While we still have 6 months to go before the election, there is no guarantee that we will ever catch him. Why blow everything up like this?"

Debbie: "I can't think of anyone else who may benefit from this."

O"Reilly: "I have to agree, the only person who might benefit would be Phil."

As they ponder this latest wrinkle, Laurie Duffy knocks on the door, opening it before waiting for the Congressman to respond: "Sorry to bother you but Senator Trooien is making a speech to the press right now. It's on every channel. I thought you needed to know."

The steam coming from the head of Bob O'Reilly is apparent to everyone: "Trooien's trying to get the jump on us. He wants to be the first to talk to the press before we can get a chance to express our feelings about the shooting."

Dan McGinnis appears to be just as irate: "I should have anticipated this. I thought he would be considerate enough to let me address the attack first, but I was wrong."

As Jake and Ava sit there with surprise looks on their faces, it's becoming more and more apparent that politics have taken over the issue.

Jake: "I guess the criminal aspect of the shooting in now on the back burner. I get the feeling that you were hoping to get first crack at the media. If I'm reading you correctly, playing the victim card might get you a bump in the polls. I guess there's more than one person who might benefit from the attack?"

Dan: "My concern with finding the shooter and ending the threat is still the most important thing. I never gave the political aspect any credence until now. I'm afraid that my opponent decided to capitalize on the attack to lessen the impact it could have on his numbers."

Ava: "Not being a savvy political operative, can you explain to me on how being first to the media could help his chances in November?"

O'Reilly: "90% percent of campaigns deal directly with the issues. The remaining 10%, which can be the difference come election night, has to do with intangibles that are hard to quantify. Do you like the candidate? Does he appear to be a good family man? Is there anything in his background that can garner sympathy, such as a troubled childhood or a handicap child? Is he a veteran that has seen action overseas?"

Debbie: "Beating your opponent by more than 10% is usually considered a blowout, therefore the intangibles can be the difference between winning and losing."

Jake: "If I read you correctly, having a shooter that almost killed Dan yesterday might be perceived as a benefit to his campaign if it can garner enough sympathy to push that 10% in his direction."

The McGinnis team realizes that their initial reaction to the speech is pushing the interview in a new direction, one that might be less conducive to their cause. The unspoken aspect of the shooting that they hope to turn in their favor is now on the table.

Dan: "I know we should be less concerned about politics right now but I can't drop my guard, even for a second. My team had nothing to do with the shooting, I can assure you of that. I would never authorize any stunt that might get someone killed or injured. While I would like to be our next Senator, it must happen because the voters thought that I was the best candidate, not because of something this dangerous."

O'Reilly: "We have been slowly gaining ground for months. Why risk everything when things are going our way for now?"

Debbie: "This whole conversation is ridiculous. Of course we had nothing to do with the shooting. If you feel otherwise, I suggest you garner some proof before insinuating that we are guilty of anything."

Jake: "We are getting way ahead of ourselves. We are not accusing you of anything. We will let the evidence take us where we need to go."

Ava, sensing that this meeting needs to end: "If any of you think of something that may help us, please let us know. I'm sorry that this happened but bad things can happen to anyone."

Ava: "Every person touched by the shooting will be looked into, including your opponent. We make no guarantees nor do we intend to allow politics to weigh into our investigation."

Jake, standing to indicate that they are leaving: "Good luck with your campaign, Congressman. I'll leave political warfare to the professionals. If we have anything that needs followup, I will touch base. Thanks for giving us the time."

As Jake and Ava leave the office, Dan, Bob and Debbie quickly turn on the TV to see what their opponent is saying. Maybe they can use some of his words against him when they speak to the press at the end of the day.

This campaign has gotten a lot more serious and a lot more combative.

Chapter Seven

The Show Must Go On

Thursday, May 9th
Phil Trooien's Residence
Bedminster, NJ - 12:13PM

After leaving the Congressman's campaign office, Jake reaches out to Kent Baldauf and Gary Ceepo, who are conducting their own interview with Senator Phil Trooien at his home.

With the call on speaker, Jake and Ava can hear a great deal of noise in the background as Kent answers the phone: "It's a mad house here, Jake. Before we could conduct the interview, Howard Clarke, the Senator's Chief of Staff, made it clear that the Senator was preparing to give a statement regarding the shooting to the press."

Trying to speak over the commotion, Gary interjects: "This is not a spontaneous speech. The press began gathering outside before we arrived more than an hour ago. They must have put this into motion as early as yesterday in order draw a crowd this size."

Jake: "Were you able to get any time with the Senator?"

74

Kent: "None at all, I'm afraid. He was secluded in his office, most likely preparing his speech, while we were being coddled by his aide, Liz Anderson. Everyone was friendly and apologetic but Phil Trooien's attention was elsewhere as he prepared his remarks for the press."

Gary: "It's hard to complain after what happened yesterday. Senator Trooien must believe that a quick response is a political necessity. If I had to guess, he wants to beat McGinnis to the microphone in order to get the press focused on him rather than the shooting."

Jake: "The political games being played never ceases to amaze me. I need you to stay around and conduct that interview, no matter how long it takes. After meeting with McGinnis, I'm more confused than ever."

Gary: "It's hard to decipher what is real and what is politics. They all play the game and the rest of us become nothing more than pawns."

Kent: "I once heard someone describe politics as being a form of organized chaos. Boy, is that the truth."

Jake: "I suggest you learn as much as you can from Phil's remarks to the press and the questions that follow. There may be insights that you can use during your interview. Call me when you're done."

As the call ends, Jake turns to Ava with a look of astonishment in his eyes: "I'm glad we have little to do with politics. The more experienced the politician, the harder it is to know what is real and what is spin."

Ava: "I'm not sure they know the difference. As for me, I always trust their actions, not their words. Anyone can promise the world if they think it will earn them votes. Unfortunately, those that **DO** rather the just **SAY** appear to be few and far between."

Five Minutes Earlier at the Senator's Home

As Phil Trooien makes his way to the microphones, he sees dozens of reporters gathered in the courtyard. This may be one of the more challenging speeches he will ever give.

There's a fine line between compassion and determination, two attributes that must be communicated to the press this afternoon. The perfect balance between the two must be accomplished if he is to succeed today. Too much determination might indicate a less than acceptable amount of compassion. Too much compassion could place all of the emphasis back on to McGinnis, increasing his chances to get the sympathy vote.

Hopefully, what they have chosen to say will strike the proper chord.

Both he and Roberta have flourished during his time in the Senate. They do not want to see that end. As for Dan McGinnis, he has been a formable opponent. Up to now, Phil has been able to keep him at bay, for the most part, but something like this can change things in a heartbeat.

This attack could not have come at a worse time for Phil. With crime skyrocketing and his crime bill mired in committee, it might appear to the untrained eye that he has turned a blind eye, which could not be further from the truth. He needs to make that point clearly and concisely, but compassionately as well.

Nobody ever said that politics is easy.

Senator Trooien steps to the microphones: "What happened yesterday in Toms River was not only tragic but unacceptable. When the shooter attempted to take the life of Dan McGinnis, he was taking aim at all of America and what we stand for, as part of the greatest nation on the planet. None of this has anything to do with politics."

Trooien: "Dan and I may be opponents in this campaign but we are not enemies. In fact, we agree on most issues, with the exception of who's best to carry them out. When someone tries to elevate that discussion with violence, we all lose."

Trooien: "This has to stop now. We need all of you in the press to spread the word that we cannot tolerate this behavior, no matter the circumstance. Violence remains the weapon of the weak, those who cannot get their point across in a civilized manner. We cannot allow the shooter to force us to bend to his wishes."

Trooien: "My heart goes out to Dan and his family. One cannot downplay what occurred nor can we minimize its impact. What we can do is support him and his family and stand by their side as the country condemns the actions of a madman."

Trooien: "I'm confident that he will be caught and punished for his actions and we will get on with our lives. Let me say that violence can never be thought of as being inevitable. We can never just accept it as being part of the fabric of our society."

Trooien: "That's why I'm pleading with my fellow Senators on the hill to pass the crime bill that I co-authored last month, which seems to have lost its way in the halls of Congress."

Trooien: "While it takes direct aim at the laws on the books that have given the criminals the benefit of the doubt rather than the victims, the bill pushes all of the sanctuary cities to reconsider their stand on illegal immigration, especially when it comes to criminal activity."

Trooien: "The men and women of Immigration and Customs Enforcement (**ICE)** are not our enemies. As for everyone who resides within our borders, no one, no matter their immigration status, deserves to be treated differently, especially when they show little regard for our laws."

Trooien: "We must face the fact that everyone let into our country are not model individuals just looking for a better life. Many of them have upped the ante on crime and they deserve none of the benefits that were put in place for the citizens of our great country. Everyone must be united on this front."

Trooien: "In addition to Dan and his family, my heart goes out to the family of officer Charlie Conroy, who remains in the hospital after bravely taking the bullet meant for the

Congressman. He represents all that is good in America and we need to reward those that put their duty ahead of their own safety. Its people like Charlie that makes us a country worth protecting."

Trooien: "With that I leave you today. This is not the right time to be discussing anything that takes us off topic. Let my remarks tell the story that needs telling. There will be plenty of time to address political issues. This is not one of them."

As he turns away from the microphones, the questions being shouted from the crowd resemble more of a word salad than they do a cogent thought.

When their cries go unanswered, the crowd begins to disperse. Articles need to be written and opinions need to be put on paper. The Senator will have to wait to find out if his efforts were well received by the voters.

As Phil heads back into his house, Gary comments on his speech: "That was a master class in political manipulation. He was tough, considerate and determined. He may have cost Dan McGinnis a few points in the polls, which I assume was the objective."

Kent: "You media types make me mad. Can't he express a real opinion without it being analyzed to death?"

Gary: "Unfortunately, we live in a world where the truth matters less than the presentation. He may have been honest in his comments but what matters is how they are perceived. On that front, he did a great job."

Kent: "I'm getting a headache just listening to you. Let's get inside and finish what we came here to do. I'm counting on you to help us fight our way through the BS. The time for political games are over. The stakes are too high."

Thursday, May 9th
McGinnis Campaign Headquarters
Middletown, NJ - 12:28PM

As Dan, Debbie and Bob are digesting Phil Trooien's latest political move, they are livid that he beat them to the punch. Dan was the victim yesterday and he should have been granted first crack at dealing with the attack.

Phil Trooien made himself a few enemies today that supersede's the campaign. While no one could pretend that politics is a bloodless sport, taking advantage of a tragedy like this is a bridge too far. Phil needed to wait his turn, which would have been the proper thing to do.

O'Reilly: "I'm going to contact the media and arrange for a proper press conference for 4:00PM. That will ensure us that the 5:00:PM evening news will have their headline, thanks to us."

Debbie: "If the questions run longer, we may find ourselves on live TV rather than on tape. Anything we can do to counter Phil's speech needs to be our focus. The voters must see Dan as being brave, fearless and committed. Everyone loves their heroes and we need to add Dan to that list."

Dan: "I have to be careful not to come off too strong or risk minimizing the attack. It was an assassination attempt that affects everyone in the state. All of New Jersey should be outraged by the attack and looking to avenge the assault by finding the shooter and putting him behind bars."

O'Reilly: "We have the added pressure of having to comment on the Senator's remarks. He was careful to be empathetic toward Dan, which requires us to do so as well. To attack him would be a mistake, in my opinion."

Dan: "It's worse than that. I'm going to have to thank him in public!"

Debbie: "We can do that without going overboard. If we put our minds together, we can find a way to diminish him in the eyes of the world while thanking him at the same time. Political rhetoric has been doing that for decades. Shake the hand of your opponent while punching him in the face with the other hand."

O'Reilly: "In this case, we have to do it better than most. Trooien's comments demand mention and any hint of politics might have the opposite affect. We have a narrow opening to climb through but it must be done."

Debbie: "Okay, we only have three hours to put together the best speech in history. I suggest we get to it."

Dan: "First things first, I need to share what happened yesterday with our campaign team outside. We have kept them in the dark and they must be on edge right now. We are going to need everyone working at a high level from this point forward. Let's put them at ease and get them properly motivated."

As all three rise and head out of the office, the most important day of the campaign is just getting started.

Thursday, May 9th
Senator Trooien's Residence
Bedminster, NJ - 12:36PM

Waiting to speak to the Senator has been especially difficult on Kent Baldauf. Patience might be a virtue but it's not high on the list of Kent's better attributes.

Kent: "I'm losing my patience, Gary. If we wait any longer, I'm not going to be responsible for my actions."

Gary: "I'm just happy to hear that you have any patience at all. I suggest you find a way to cope before we get inside. We're meeting with a Senator, not an uncooperative witness. The last thing you want to do is have to explain to Jake how you blew our interview to bits. Just take a deep breath and think of anything that can calm you down."

Kent, with a sly smile on his face: "Like emptying my pistol at the driving range. I could place a picture of Trooien on the target."

Just then, Howard Clarke opens the door to the Senator's office, greeting Gary and Kent, inviting them in: "Sorry for the delay. Phil can see you now."

As they sit down, Phil Trooien rises from his seat to greet them properly: "I'm really sorry that I've held you up this long. This has been a crazy day. All the plans we had for today were blown apart by yesterday's shooting."

Gary: "We understand, Senator. What's important right now is finding the shooter as quickly as possible. We just have a few questions and then we will let you get back to your day."

Trooien: "Ask away."

Kent, not waiting for Gary to interject: "In your opinion Senator, what did Dan McGinnis do or say that led to yesterday's shooting?"

Trooien: "I'm not sure what you mean by that? How would I know what led to the attack?"

Kent: "When a politician is targeted, you have to expect that it's related to his or her political persona. You being his opponent, what positions did Dan get behind that might have led to the shooting? How does his views differ from yours?"

Howard Clarke feels the need to interject before the interview strays too far from center: "There has been nothing politically that could justify such an attack. We share more than we disagree with, which makes this less political and more personal, in my opinion."

Gary, talking directly to the Chief of Staff: "No matter how hard you try to pretend that a senate campaign can remain civilized by just nibbling around the edges of issues, a candidate will not secure enough votes by playing it safe. That might work for the incumbent, if they are in the lead, but not the other party. What issue has Dan selected to separate himself from your position that might sway the voters to his side?"

Trooien, seeing Howard Clarke's frustration: "This conversation is heading in the wrong direction. I want to cooperate, not become an obstacle, to your investigation. For argument's sake, if we assume the shooter targeted Dan for political reasons, his take on crime, as well as terrorism, could be perceived as points of contention."

Trooien: "I use the term perceived because we really are, for the most part, on the same page. Dan considers my efforts to be feckless in that regard, which offers him a chance to sway voters in his direction. My proposed legislation is far from toothless. If I am able to get my crime bill passed, Dan's main point of contention would vanish."

Roberta Trooien is outside the door to Phil's home office, debating as to whether she should interject herself into the middle of the discussion. Phil has always depended on her for advice, especially when it comes to issues of the heart.

While he can be too objective at times, Roberta constantly reminds him that such an approach might be viewed as being a little too cold and displaced. His constituents need to see that he can be empathetic as well, which goes a long way in having them believe that he cares about an issue rather than just being able to understand it.

As she hears Phil objectifying this crisis, she decides to enter the fray.

Roberta starts to knock on the door, while simultaneously entering the office, carrying a glass of water: "I'm sorry gentlemen for the intrusion but Phil needs to take his blood pressure medicine which, based on what I was able to overhear, could not come at a better time."

As she smiles at everyone, she places the glass on the desk with the pill wrapped in a napkin. Roberta decides to continue: "When I first talked to Phil after the shooting, he was beside himself with shock and concern, not just for Dan but for everyone in the park."

Roberta: "He understood the sense of horror and fear that must have emanated from the crowd and the confusion that everyone must have felt as to how such a thing could happen?"

Roberta: "Phil has always had difficulty expressing his emotions. Deep down inside I suspect he sees the showing of emotion to be a frailty rather than an asset. I'm constantly reminding him that showing real emotion is not a weakness. Maybe someday, he will believe me."

Phil, smiling and addressing Kent and Gary: "When all is said and done, politicians do not succeed in a vacuum. While Howie has always been the person looking forward, always analyzing the direction the wind is blowing, Roberta has kept me grounded and humble so as not to let this Senatorial thing go to my head."

Howie: "The truth is that the best politicians understand the need for balance. That goes beyond legislation to include communication. Don't talk over the people, talk to them. Phil's success lies in his humanity as much as his political prowess."

Gary: "I could not agree more. Overseers who preach to the public quickly wear out their welcome, not a good longterm strategy."

Kent: "While I'm, most likely, the least political person in the room, our team has been assigned the responsibility of finding the shooter before they hurt anyone else. In order to do that, we have to interview everyone that may have insight into who the shooter is or why the shooter acted the way they did, which includes you and your team."

Phil: "I understand why you are here and if I can do anything to help you find this guy, I pledge to do so. With that said, I'm not sure how I can help? The events of yesterday were as much a surprise to me as it was to the rest of the country. I can't imagine anyone willing to kill Dan for political reasons. Is it possible that the attack could have been personal?"

Gary: "It's too early to rule out anything at the moment but politics must remain center stage for now. We find it hard to believe that a shooter with a personal grievance would attempt this at a rally where there are hundreds of people and dozens of law enforcement near by. The risk of getting caught is far greater at a rally unless the message being sent had a political angle that needed to be expressed."

Roberta, feeling the need to make a point, decides to speak up: "While I never interfere with Phil's political campaign or his political stance on any of the issues, I cannot help but notice that the shooter missed his target."

Roberta: "It's no secret that Dan was behind in the polls since the beginning of his campaign. Could his campaign benefit from a failed attempt on his life?"

Phil, showing outrage at her comment: "Roberta, that'a a terrible thing for you to say. A security guard was badly wounded yesterday and it is inconceivable to me that Dan would ever pull a stunt like that!"

Roberta: "Phil, you are missing the point. I find it just as inconceivable but if there is a connection to politics, choosing to keep your head in the sand is not constructive."

Gary: "Roberta is right, we need to consider all possibilities. Short of the shooter being a random crazy, who benefits from the attack? Could Dan see a jump in the polls after having survived such an attack?"

Howard Clarke takes no time to answer the question: "Absolutely he could benefit. There is a common thread when it comes to the sympathy vote, that's why candidates always discuss tragedies in their life or the lives of other family members. Feeling sorry for someone can be the difference maker at times. I suspect having someone trying to kill you would be a significant sympathy card to play."

Phil: "I'm having difficulty getting behind this. This is a far cry from talking about a son with a drug problem or the death of a spouse from cancer."

Kent: "If we are to put all of our cards on the table, is there a chance you could benefit from the shooting as well?"

Phil: "I can't see how? The media's focus, at least for the near future, will be on Dan McGinnis. That gives him an audience that would have never been there except for the attack. We will see what the polls say but politically, things appear to be in his favor."

Clarke: "I can't foresee us getting a bump in the polls, the momentum favors McGinnis."

Clarke: "In fact, we are caught between a rock and a hard place. Being too aggressive right now will appear to be less than sympathetic. Being too soft could add to his favorable numbers. This is not an enviable position for us to be in."

Gary: "I must say you took a major step today in countering the narrative. The Senator's speech was short and to the point, not an easy task. In my opinion, I'd say your team walked that tightrope perfectly. Being first to address the media was a brilliant political strategy."

Phil: "We had to do the best with the hand we were dealt. How successful it turns out to be is anyone's guess."

Kent: "I'm not so sure that earning political points is all on the side of the Congressman. I learned today that your crime bill was collecting dust in the Senate before yesterday. Having such a glaring reminder for everyone on how violent our society has become might just be the added push you need to get the bill passed."

Gary: "McGinnis decided that crime and terrorism would be the key talking points for his campaign. I would think that you could punch a very large hole into his campaign by getting your Crime Bill resurrected from the ashes to the Senate floor for a vote."

Phil: "Are you insinuating that I would place my opponent in harm's way just to get a bill passed?"

Gary: "All I'm saying is that the potential for a political benefit from the shooting is not limited to one side. We need to consider everything right now. If our team is to solve this, we cannot afford to leave any door unopened."

Roberta: "I'm sorry I brought any of this up. The last thing I wanted was to have either party linked to such a heinous attack. Politics may be ruthless at times but this is so far out of bounds for any of this to be politically motivated."

Kent: "We will be looking into everyone with a connection to Dan and his campaign."

Kent: "Please don't take our investigation personally. My experience tells me that the shooting is not a one and done. There will be more coming and we may not get away next time without a fatality or multiple fatalities. We have to find the shooter quickly before anyone else gets hurt."

As things settle down, its obvious to everyone in the room that The New Jersey Special Projects Task Force will not take sides nor will they let anything get in the way of capturing the shooter.

Those who have nothing to hide will be best served by cooperating in any way possible.

After today's meeting, Phil Trooien is painfully aware that no one is free from scrutiny, including a sitting United State Senator.

Chapter Eight

It's a World of Smoke and Mirrors

Thursday, May 9th
Habib Residence
Fairfield, NJ - 1:46PM

As Josef Habib, along with his fellow jihadists, are strategizing about their upcoming attempt on Jake Patrick's life, his burner phone rings, indicating that their benefactor is on the other end.

As Josef places a finger to his lips, asking for silence, he connects the call with his phone on speaker before responding: "I was waiting to hear from you. There appears to be a significant amount of chaos from yesterday's shooting, which was our intent all along. You should be pleased."

Benefactor: "The reaction to the shooting appears to be more complicated than I expected it to be. By injuring the security guard you upped the ante, increasing the odds that the investigators will be more diligent in their pursuit of the shooter."

Benefactor: "For some reason, the governor decided to put Jake Patrick and his team in charge of the investigation, which is not ideal, if you ask me. Their track record is impressive and I was hoping to avoid this much scrutiny until we finished the job."

Josef: "You're worrying about nothing. As a matter of fact, I made sure that Jake Patrick would be involved in the case and my plan worked perfectly."

Benefactor: "You did what? Why the hell did you do that? The last thing we want is having a national hero look into this. What you did was inexcusable and dangerous. I'm not paying you to improvise, just to do what you are being paid to do."

Josef, trying to temper his rage before speaking: "If you thought I was going to follow your advice to the letter, you were mistaken. It's my life in the balance, not yours. I left a few clues behind to indicate a possible terror connection to the shooting. I wanted the

authorities to go off in the wrong direction long enough for us to complete the assignment. That's exactly what appears to be happening."

Benefactor: "I think you are underestimating his task force but the damage is done, there's little we can do about that now."

Benefactor: "I want you to implement phase two this afternoon. Dan McGinnis has called a press conference in front of the Governor's office in Trenton to address the attack. You need to disrupt that press conference. This time, don't go off on your own. I want no one hurt. A warning shot is all that is required."

Josef: "This is why I cannot let you handle the details. The security at the press conference will be substantial. If I'm to get away safely, you must allow me to improvise."

Benefactor: "How so?"

Josef: "The shot will happen after the press conference as he makes his way back to his office, someplace that is not overrun with security. I will make sure it has the necessary impact and no one will get hurt, but I'm doing it my way."

The benefactor, hesitating a little before responding: "Okay, just get it done."

As the call ends, Josef turns to his team: "I'm going to need your help to pull this off. Alaina, I need you to head to the Congressman's office in Middletown and follow his car to the press conference. We have to know what route they plan on taking. I suspect the return trip will follow a similar path."

Josef: "Mohammed, you will need to arrange to have your truck stationed along the route to run interference, just enough to slow his car down, giving me time to activate my plan."

Josef: "Abdul, I need you to be my weapon."

Josef: "After this attack, Jake Patrick will have to play a more active role in protecting the Congressman from harm. That's how we will be able to better monitor his movements and arrange for his demise, which needs to be powerful enough to leave nothing to chance."

Thursday, May 9th
Office of the NJ Special Projects Task Force
Morristown, NJ - 3:02PM

After a busy morning, all members of the task force are back in the office. Its time to shed some light on their findings while everything is fresh in their minds.

While the rest of the team were conducting interviews, Tricia Highland was meeting with her muslim informants. If there is a terror connection, someone may have heard or seen something that could be of help.

Jake: "I don't know how everyone else feels after our interviews, but I'm more confused than ever. Rather than narrowing down our suspect list, I find things going in the opposite direction."

Kent: "You're not alone on that front. I got the feeling that the Senator and his Chief of Staff were prepared to say just about anything that could distance themselves from the shooting."

Jake: "Before we get into the political interviews, I'd like to hear from Tricia."

Tricia, after scouring her notes: "As far as chatter goes, no one I interviewed heard anything out of the ordinary. There were no warning signs."

Jake: "What type of warning signs?"

Tricia: "Radicals begin spending a great amount of time with a select group of people, ignoring the rest of the attendees. Sometimes they fail to keep a regular schedule or they begin showing up at odd times."

Tricia: "The mosque has always been the center of activity for many muslims, especially those that favor a more aggressive interpretation of the Koran."

Kent: "All muslims are not religious zealots. That would suggest that all radicals might not be among the overly religious as well. What if the terrorist cell we are looking for is part of the latter? I doubt any of your contacts would even know who they are?"

Tricia: "That might be true but I have yet to encounter a radical that does not follow a strict religious code."

Jake: "So, I assume, you found nothing that might suggest that an active terror cell was in the making?"

Tricia: "As it became apparent to me that we were not going to get that lucky, I pushed my contacts for anything that might be considered out of the ordinary, no matter how trivial it may appear to be."

Tricia: "That question led to the Iman from the EL SHARIA Mosque in Paterson to share a concern that he considered unusual."

Tricia: "He noticed one of his members breaking their patterned behavior the last few weeks. His name is Abdul Farouk. He owns the local muslim religious store downtown and comes to the mosque two nights a week. He has missed two services in the last 10 days and when the Iman visited his store to buy a few things yesterday, he was not there."

Gary: "Is that so unusual? There could be a dozen reasons he was not in his store."

Tricia: "According to the Iman, his whole life revolves around running the store and attending services. Even though it does not appear to be that significant, the Iman thought it important enough to share it with me."

Kent: "I have to agree with Gary on this one. I'm sure the Iman wanted to help so he dug deep to provide you with something. This does not seem like odd behavior to me."

Jake: "My instincts tell me that the terror angle is still worth pursuing. With nothing else to go on I suggest we look into this guy. We all know that every lead doesn't have a neon sign pointing us in the right direction. Let's see what we can dig up."

Jake: "As for our interview today with Congressman McGinnis, I'll let Ava bring you up to speed."

Ava: "While I could tell that the Congressman was shaken by the attack and the office staff a little disoriented, the campaign was proceeding without a hitch. McGinnis appeared to be more concerned about his poll numbers than he was with being the target of an assassin."

Gary: "Sympathy can be a powerful motivator. I suspect that a failed shooting could provide a gold mine of sympathy for Dan."

Ava: "I wasn't looking in that direction but anything's possible."

Jake, turning toward Kent and Gary: "What did you learn from the meeting with the Senator?"

Kent: "Senator Trooien tried to take the high road but his actions this morning suggested otherwise. The speech he gave to condemn the attack and offer sympathy

to McGinnis was carefully thought out and planned in advance, probably right after the shooting."

Gary: "Being first in front of the media was an attempt to soften the blow and minimize any bump McGinnis was hoping to achieve."

Kent: "If the shooting might favor the victim politically, doesn't that tell us that it is less likely that Senator Trooien and his campaign had anything to do with the attack?"

Gary: "Normally I would agree with you, but we cannot forget the crime bill he proposed to the Senate. If passed, it could upend McGinnis's campaign strategy of depicting Trooien as being ineffective."

Jake: "Okay, let's see where we stand. We have two political opponents who might benefit from the shooting in some way. Both campaigns appear to be more focused on advancing their political future than they are on finding the person or persons responsible for yesterday's attack."

Jake: "We have a shooter that tried a little too hard to convince us that terrorism was responsible for the shooting. All that accomplished was getting us assigned to the case."

Gary: "We are back to where we started. In my opinion, I can see only two reasons the shooter chose to highlight the terrorism angle. He either wanted to throw out a red herring that sends us off on a wild goose chase or he wanted to make sure that our team was put in charge of the investigation."

Kent: "We are beginning to talk in circles. Where does this leave us?"

Jake: "We have to account for both. As for the political angle, Gary, Ava and I will try to make sense of things while Tricia and Kent will stay on the terror angle. You guys can start with looking into this Abdul fellow. I know its not much but it's all we have at the moment."

Jake is a little apprehensive about splitting the team. They work best when the team is focused on a single objective, but sometimes, you have to play the hand you're dealt.

Thursday, May 9ᵗʰ
Josef Habib's Residence
Fairfield, NJ - 3:19PM

_____

As Habib is patiently waiting to hear from his team, he feels a mixture of excitement and trepidation. The plan he put together is a good one. While he prefers to be part of the implementation, this second strike needs to occur without him.

While lost in thought, his phone rings: "Alaina, have you determined the most likely route for the Congressman?"

Alaina: "I believe so. While most of the trip is highway, there is a two mile stretch that offers us an opportunity to strike. When leaving the turnpike heading back to his office, he must navigate a number of neighborhood streets before reaching Route 33, a multi-lane road with a great deal of traffic. We have the best chance if we hit him before he reaches Route 33."

As Josef is studying a local street map while listening to Alaina: "I will have Abdul place the explosives about three quarters of the way down Majestic Ave., one of the street they need to travel. It will be his responsibility to set off the explosion and it will be Mohammed's responsibility to provide the necessary obstacle."

Alaina: "After the press conference, I will follow behind the Congressman's car to insure they follow the planned route. Do not worry Josef, we will take care of everything."

Josef: "I know you will do us proud. Call me when its over."

Thursday, May 9th
Outside the Governor's Mansion
Trenton, NJ - 3:58PM

―――――――――――――――

Dan McGinnis cannot shake how anxious he is facing the press for the first time since the shooting. Once again, he's outdoors but in a secure location that offers little opportunity for another attack. While that should ease his concerns, the sense of dread that is emanating from every pore remains overpowering.

It's obvious that the shooting affected him more than he realized. He must control his emotions or this speech will be a disaster.

Though he had a chance to practice his speech a number of times over the past few hours, it's not the words that matter, if his state of mind suggests anything other than

strength and determination. If Dan's anxiety is on display, nothing he says will hit home. All they will remember is how rattled he was after yesterday's shooting.

As the Congressman makes his way to the podium, he reaches down into his core, taking a deep breath before beginning one of the more important speeches in his political life. There will be no second chances.

As the crowd quiets down, Dan steps in front of the microphones: "In the first few seconds after the shot rang out and Charlie Conroy fell to the ground in pain, I was both confused and terrified. My instincts told me to hit the ground before the next shot could find its mark."

Dan: "While lying on the ground, I was relieved as the second shot never materialized."

Dan: "Before I could gather my thoughts, I was left with a sense of relief that was overshadowed by an equally strong sense of guilt. That should be me on the ground writhing in pain? Why was I spared?"

Dan: "I can only surmise that it was my aggressive stance on crime, that led to the shooting, one that resulted in officer Conroy paying the price for my political views. The shooter wanted to end my life but Charlie intervened, for that I will be forever grateful."

Dan: "As a country, we have failed to foster an atmosphere of responsibility for one's actions. Today, criminals have been emboldened by our soft approach on crime, believing that their actions will go unpunished. This has got to stop. We are a nation of laws and we have those laws for a reason."

Dan: "Those who exhibit sociopathic tendencies will not change their ways because we extended them an olive branch in the form of leniency. Doing so will only result in more crime, not less."

Dan: "The thief who robs a store one day and gets off scot free, may turn out to be the thief that kills the store owner tomorrow. He has to pay for robbing the store in the first place, that's the only way we can prevent future crimes from occurring. Every criminal is not just stealing a loaf of bread to feed their family. Making that assumption can only lead to more chaos on our streets."

Dan: "I will not rest until we place our law abiding citizens above all else. No one should have to fear leaving their homes or walking our streets. In an effort to avoid that isolated case where an innocent person winds up behind bars, we have put the rest of us in danger."

Dan: "The world's a complicated place. There are no simple answers. What I do know is that we are capable of doing two things at once. Let's find a way to avoid mistakes without allowing known criminals a free pass to wreak havoc on a law abiding society."

Dan: "I want to thank Senator Trooien for his kind words this morning. Neither one of us can afford to be looking over our shoulders, afraid that someone who might disagree with our position on any topic feels emboldened to act out in an aggressive manner."

Dan: "Phil and I can disagree on issues but never on principle. We may joke at times about politics being a bloodsport but that's as far as it goes."

Dan: "As for my campaign going forward, I will not let this interfere with how I approach the upcoming election. I'm in it for the long haul and no crazed gunman is going to make me alter my plans."

Dan: "If you have any questions, this is the time for you to ask."

As Dan allows himself to breath freely again, he takes this momentary break to compose himself and allow politics to, once again, take center stage.

As he falls back into campaign mode, he can feel it in his bones. His desire to be the next Senator is alive and well.

Chapter Nine

Bombs Away

Thursday, May 9th
Inside the Car of Congressman McGinnis
On Route to Middletown, NJ - 4:51PM

As the Chevy Suburban departs the Governor's mansion, on route to Dan's campaign headquarters, the passengers inside are feeling a sense of relief. Dan and his wife Debbie are in the back seat while Bob O'Reilly is riding up front with the driver.

O'Reilly: "I'm impressed Dan, you really pulled yourself together. From my vantage point, I saw no hesitation or uncertainty emanating from you at all. You projected strength and determination, just the way we planned it."

Debbie: "Bob's right, I could not be prouder of you. Nothing about your remarks came off as being political. It was short, sincere and to the point. You even managed to thank Phil without overdoing it, choosing to avoid comparisons with his stance on the issues. We will get a favorable bump in the polls, I can feel it."

Dan: "I'm not sure that the two of you are objective enough to comment on my demeanor. Before facing the microphones, I was seconds away from running in the other direction. It took everything I had to remain at the podium."

Debbie: "Well, whatever you did to calm yourself was not noticeable."

O'Reilly: "We may be partisan but we are not stroking your ego. You were great."

Dan: "Let's hope the media agrees with you. If we were able to win them over, the public will follow their lead."

As the car continues on its journey, the three passengers have no idea what lies in store for them.

Thursday, May 9th
Majestic Ave.
10 miles West of Middletown, NJ - 5:09PM

————————————————

With the temperature in the mid seventies and the sky a solid blue, not a cloud in sight, the local residents are moving about with smiles on their faces and an extra bounce in their steps.

For a brief second, Abdul Farouk is lamenting the damage that is about to reign down on this neighborhood. While collateral damage has always been a part of war, such attacks rarely occur in a place that is so far removed from the battlefield.

He quickly dismisses such thoughts as he has job to do, one that he intends to complete successfully. In the next few minutes, all thoughts that the attack on the Congressman might be a one and done event will dissipate, tossed into the bin of forgotten theories.

As Farouk waits, with the remote firmly in his hand, his fellow jihadists are doing their part to ensure that today's explosion will take place according to plan. Alaina Assis is tracking the Congressman's car and Mohammed Sarif has his truck positioned properly for the crucial role he is to play.

As the Congressman continues his journey, he's just minutes away from playing an important role in the demise of Jake Patrick.

Today, Josef Habib will not be the only jihadist who rises to the challenge. All of their names will be talked about with reverence among their fellow BAHRUN loyalists. After today, they will be one step closer to sending Jake Patrick to the gates of hell.

As Abdul patiently waits for the perfect time to detonate the bomb, he prays to Allah, offering himself up as a soldier in his army.

Thursday, May 9th
Inside the Car of Congressman McGinnis
On Route to Middletown, NJ - 5:14PM

————————————————

As they make their way back to the office, Dan, Debbie and Bob are planning their next move. How best can they use the events of yesterday to bolster greater support for their campaign?

All they are deep into their discussion, the car breaks quickly, throwing everyone forward by the sudden loss of movement. The driver curses under his breath and then apologizes to his passengers: "I'm sorry about that, that stupid truck in front of us just turned without looking. I'm starting to wonder if the driver even has a valid license?"

As they shake off the temporary interruption, the truck appears to be taking the same route, as he signals for a left turn on Majestic. The annoyance on the face of Dan's driver is noticeable.

As the truck driver reaches the intersection, he begins his turn a little too slowly for everyone's liking. Then, without warning, the truck stops dead in the road, blocking the street and forcing everyone behind him to come to a stop.

Dan's Driver: "Now what's wrong? The truck is blocking the road ahead of us and it looks like the driver is getting out of the vehicle."

O'Reilly: "He looks as if there's something wrong with the truck."

Dan's Driver, showing his annoyance, opens the door to exit the car: "Maybe I can help him find the problem."

Before he can exit the car, a huge explosion occurs just around the corner on Majestic that rocks their car severely. The noise and the aftershock is so intense, that everyone drops to the floor of the vehicle, looking for some protection from God knows what!

As the shock dissipates and the deafening noise is replaced with silence, they all slowly lift themselves up from the floor of the car. What they see in front of them is a bit surreal, though not unexpected.

There's a great deal of debris in the air as a fire rages just out of view, most likely coming from the site of the explosion. The truck driver, who is lying on the ground next to his truck, is slowly getting off the ground, holding his ears and staggering away from the explosion. He's covered in ash but appears to be unharmed, at least physically.

Within seconds, the silence is broken as screams of horror and pain fill the air. With the streets crowded, the casualties will be numerous. Dan's driver decides to see if he can help. As he exits the car, the truck driver staggers and falls onto the hood of the Congressman's car, crying and praying at the same time.

Dan's Driver: "Are you all right?"

Truck Driver (Mohammed Sarif): "I don't know what happened? My truck stalled as I was turning the corner. I'm not a mechanic but I knew I could not get it to move. As I was about to call my company, the explosion occurred, throwing me to the ground. I thought for sure that I was a goner."

Dan's Driver: "If you made that turn we both may have been goners. Whatever caused the explosion would have happened with both of us a lot closer to the blast. As strange as it sounds, we may owe our lives to your breakdown."

As the sounds of sirens can be heard in the distance, Dan, Debbie and Bob all exit the car, getting a better view of the damage to the neighborhood. They can see a number of wounded people staggering about, trying to get themselves farther away from ground zero.

The looks on their faces do not require verbal clarification. Was this a tragic accident or was it an intentional act aimed to silence the Congressman?

McGinnis cannot help assume the latter. The blast occurred within seconds of the truck stalling in front of them. If the vehicles proceeded as expected, it's not a stretch to believe that the blast was meant for him, especially after yesterday's attack. The anxiety he so desperately tried to alleviate, appears to be back.

As they wait the arrival of the authorities, Dan can only pray that he is wrong and the blast was a result of some random event, such as a gas explosion. If it was intentional, he can only surmise that the shooter has upped his game and that does not bode well for him.

Dan can't help wonder if his desire to be Senator is worth it? He must decide if continuing his campaign is worth the risk to his life, something that never crossed his mind until now.

Thursday, May 9th
Office of the NJ Special Projects Task Force
Morristown, NJ - 5:41PM

Kent and Tricia, who were put in charge of investigating the possibility of a terror connection, have put together a plan of action on the terror front.

Kent will use his governmental contacts, in both the CIA and the FBI, to see if Abdul Farouk is on any of their watch lists, or associated with anyone that they consider to be questionable.

Tricia will pretend to be a member of a lesser known mosque, looking to buy supplies from Abdul's store in Paterson. Approaching him from a business perspective might help her gain his trust in a non-threatening way.

As Kent waits to hear back from the intelligence community, the news on TV is leading with a story about an explosion taking place a few miles west of Middletown.

Kent, always focused on terror related events, turns up the volume before making another call. Hopefully, there's a logical explanation for the blast.

While Jake, Ava and Gary are gathered in the conference room, they see the same breaking news story on the TV. As they listen to the reporter describe the event, Gary is the first to respond: "It has to be a gas explosion. The damage is significant, which means the blast was substantial. The only thing I can think of with that much power would be gas."

Ava: "It looks really bad. I'm afraid the casualties will be significant. I just recently converted my home from gas to electric. I know the bills will be higher but the number of gas accidents in the past year had me concerned."

Meanwhile, Kent has muted the TV once again and is on the phone with one of his contacts at the NSA. As he's providing his contact with the name of the store owner, he glances up at the TV, only to see that Congressman Daniel McGinnis is on the screen, looking less like a politician and more like a victim.

Kent: "Jim, somethings come up, I'm going to have to go. See what you can find on this Farouk guy. Call me if you have anything."

As the phone call ends, Kent unmutes the TV to learn that Dan's car was close enough to the blast to do some real damage. As he heads out to inform the rest of the team about the explosion, he finds all three if his team members staring at the TV with the sound turned up.

Jake: "This cannot be a coincidence."

_____

On the TV, the reporter is talking to the Congressman: "Are you telling me Congressman that your car was seconds away from being closer to the blast?"

McGinnis: "We were very lucky. If that truck in front of us did not stall at the turn, we would have followed him down the street, placing us in immediate danger. Sometimes luck can be your best friend."

McGinnis: "My concern is for all of the people who were not that lucky. This is a tragedy of massive proportions. While I suspect this is an accident, if anyone's negligence is responsible for the blast, they must face the consequences. Do you know anything about the casualties as of yet?"

Reporter: "All I know is that there are significant fatalities. The blast appears to have originated from a car parked on the street but that is not an official declaration by the authorities. It's too soon for anything definitive."

Reporter: "This is especially troublesome for you, Congressman. Being involved in two deadly incidents in less than two days must be disconcerting, don't you think?"

McGinnis: "I can't worry about that right now. My thoughts are with those who suffered the most today." With that said, Dan turns away from the reporter as he heads back to his car.

Off camera, Bob O"Reilly, who was talking to the investigator in charge, returns to the car as well with welcomed news: "We are free to leave."

————————————————————————

Gary: "This might not be an accident. If the reporter is correct, a car could never cause that much damage unless it was altered in some way. Someone would have had to intentionally turn it into a bomb."

Gary: "In my opinion, we cannot wait for the final report on the explosion. If the Congressman is being targeted, he could be dead before the report is released."

Ava: "There's no way the Congressman was just in the wrong place at the wrong time. I say we treat it as an intentional act, not an accident. Whoever placed that bomb was looking to kill or injure the Congressman. We need to look into the truck driver as well. Did his truck stall or did he stop intentionally? I'm not big on coincidences."

Jake: "I'll call the governor right away. We need to talk to the head investigator and get his notes immediately. Once the governor knows that this might be connected to our investigation, I'm sure everyone will cooperate."

Kent: "Until we find out more, I'm having difficulty understanding the bomb, assuming it turns out to be one."

Kent: "The facts don't add up. If the blast went off prematurely, you would have to assume the delay in making the turn resulted in the failed attempt on the Congressman. That would mean the bomb was on a timer."

Kent: "The use of a timer makes no sense whatsoever. Too many variables exist to perfectly time the arrival of the Congressman's car. It can only work by having the bomber set off the blast remotely."

Jake: "I agree with Kent. There's no way the blast could be on a timer."

Jake: "If someone set it off via remote, it only makes sense if the blast was designed to scare McGinnis rather than to kill him. It would follow a similar path as the shooting."

Kent: "The shooter had an easy shot that he failed to execute. If his plan was to frighten the Congressman, not kill him, the same could be said for the bombing."

Ava: "That might explain the shooting for me but not the bombing. If this whole mess centers on a political attempt to influence an election, I can understand scaring him at the rally but not today. When the final casualty report is released, we may have dozens of people killed and dozens more injured. That level of escalation suggests terrorism, not political discourse."

Gary: "I have to agree. Escalating to mass murder seems out of character for anyone concerned about an election. Maybe the clues left behind were not decoys at all. We have to take the terror angle seriously."

Kent: "That leaves us with one possible lead to follow. I wish it was a little more promising."

As Jake glances at the TV, he sees a reporter talking to a middle eastern man about the blast. He asks everyone to quiet down as he raises the volume: "I want to see who this guy is. His name flashed quickly but it was definitely middle eastern."

Reporter: "The Congressman thinks that you may have saved his life. What made you stop your truck from entering the street?"

Mohammed Sarif: "All of a sudden I lost power, why I do not know. The engine just stopped working. I was about to call my company when the blast occurred. All I could think about at that moment was that I was blocking the road and their were going to be a lot of angry people."

Reporter: "Did you know that Congressman McGinnis was in the car behind you?"

Sarif: "I had no idea. When the blast knocked me to the ground, I thought I was going to die. As I started to recover, I headed farther away from the blast, which was purely instinct. I wound up in front of his car."

Showing some emotion after the trauma, he finishes his thought: "We are both alive purely by chance. God was looking out for us, I guess?"

Reporter: "Thank you, Mr. Sarif. I appreciate you giving us a few minutes to tell your story."

As the station went to commercial, Jake turned down the volume once again.

Jake: "We now have two suspects to investigate. That truck prevented the Congressman's car from entering the street. It also kept the truck out of harm's way. If

the blast was designed to frighten Dan, the truck could be the prime reason he is not in the morgue right now."

Ava: "At least we have another angle to work on. As for the Congressman, how do you want to handle him? I think we need to play a bigger part, if not take control of his security."

Jake: "I agree with Ava. I want Kent on his detail. His skillset and instincts are the best among our team members and that makes him the perfect candidate."

Jake: "Kent and I will leave immediately for Dan's campaign office. I want no phones calls, no requests for a meeting and no advanced warning. We need to talk to him and his team unabridged and unprepared. How this latest setback has affected them is a key to understanding where their heads are at."

Ava: "I'll touch base with Tricia letting her know of the change. I'll help her on the investigative front. We now have a second possible suspect in the trucker. If we can tie the two of them together, everything else might fall into place."

Gary: "Before we break this up, I need to clear the air on a few things. I'm more convinced than ever that our answers will not be found in one direction. This is not one or the other, but both."

Gary: "There is someone, or a number of people on the political front, that wanted to throw a monkey wrench into this campaign. Whether to bolster a candidate in the polls or to send a campaign off the rails, the reason the attacks occurred on a political candidate is not an accident."

Gary: "There's also little doubt, in my mind, that there is a terror connection. The bombing today convinced me of that. No one kills dozens of people to scare a candidate away from running, unless that person has no regard for human life."

Gary: "How a political ploy to interfere with an election morphed into terrorism is still a mystery but we are looking for two distinct perpetrators. I can't help feel that our involvement in this case is the reason for the terror connection. Why would a terror cell care about the campaign for Senator? They must be using the politicians in order to get to us."

Jake: "I cannot disagree with you. The more we examine the evidence, I'm more inclined to believe that a political figure has chosen to join forces with a terrorist. The quicker we discover who the political operative is, the better the chance we have of crumbling the entire threat."

Politics is now front and center in a terror investigation. For the first time, Jake and his team find themselves swimming in unfamiliar waters.

Chapter Ten

_____

Where do we go from here?

Thursday, May 9th
The Home of Senator Trooien
Bedminster, NJ - 6:12PM

_____

Senator Phil Trooien, and his wife Roberta, were looking forward to a quiet evening at home. All of that came to an end when the news led with the blast that occurred in central New Jersey. Seeing a reporter interviewing Congressman McGinnis at the scene told the both of them that this was more than just a random coincidence.

Usually the TV is on when Phil and Roberta are having dinner, providing them with familiar background noise. Tonight its soft dinner music, designed to sooth their minds, so that they can eat in peace, letting the world pass by without incident. As the old saying goes, *Ignorance is Bliss.*

Before taking their first bite, Howard Clarke decides to call with news of the blast. While Phil is tempted to let it ring, he cannot bring himself to send the message to voicemail.

In the few seconds it takes Phil to answer the call, Howie begins ranting about the bombing and its obvious connection to Dan McGinnis. After this second attack in as many days, someone is intent on disrupting Dan's life, if not ending it.

Phil, turning to Roberta: "Howie will be here shortly. He feels we need to get ahead of this before we have to answer questions from the press."

Tonight's dinner will have to wait.

As Phil and Roberta prepare for Howie's arrival, their conversation turns to the obvious: "Roberta, this is a complicated issue that must be handled properly. I have to place politics on the back burner for now or I will come across as an opportunist, which will not bode well for the re-election campaign."

Roberta: "I understand your concerns, but in my humble opinion, the best course of action is to say nothing at all. You addressed yesterday's shooting with the media, which was appropriate. Until there is a definitive explanation for the blast, to assume the two events are connected is a path you do not want to take."

Phil: "Why do you say that?"

Roberta: "In a world where everything seems to be political, you get one chance to play the sympathy card without reprisal from the press. You played that card this morning."

Roberta: "What if the blast turns out to be accidental? Any comment you make prematurely will not sit well with the voters. If the press asks you to comment, tell them that this is an ongoing investigation and it serves no productive purpose to weigh in when there is nothing of value you can offer."

Phil, smiling as he looks at Roberta: "Maybe its time to fire Howie and make you the Chief of Staff? You are the heart that is needed right now. My analytical approach to things might make things worse, especially if I come across as being uncaring."

Roberta: "Don't be ridiculous, I'm no politician. I'm just a caring wife who looks after Phil Trooien, not the Senator. I'm just reminding you that this may not be the time for you to be factual rather than emotional, that's all."

As the doorbell rings and Roberta opens the door for Howard Clarke, she guides him into the living room: "I'll leave you boys alone for now. If you want anything, just let me know."

As Roberta leaves the room, Phil turns to Howie and says: "We can analyze this to death if we want but I'm going to remain in the background for now. We cannot comment without risking blowback."

Howie: "Are you sure about this? Getting another opportunity for broad media exposure does not come around that often."

Phil: "Whether it helps us or hurts us politically, we have to let Dan take the lead on this. He's the one in the line of fire, not us. To take advantage of this to increase my exposure is both unethical and politically dangerous."

Phil: "My mind is made up, Howie. We remain on the sidelines for now."

Thursday, May 9th
Campaign Office of Dan McGinnis
Middletown, NJ - 6:51PM

As Jake and Kent arrive at the campaign office, they can see the lights are still on in the back. The front bullpen area is dark, indicating that the support staff has all left for the day.

As Jake dials the Congressman's cellphone, Dan answers on the second ring: "Mr. Patrick, I can guess why you're calling but could we possibly touch base tomorrow? I could really use a break right now."

Jake: "I'm afraid we need to talk tonight, when everything is still fresh in your mind. I've learned, over the years, that traumatic events are best discussed right away before details begin to erode."

Dan: "I was hoping to spend the evening with my family. Getting back on the road right now seems like a big ask. Are you sure we can't wait until tomorrow?"

Jake: "There's no need for you to get on the road. In fact, both myself and Kent Baldauf are standing in front of your campaign office. All you have to do it open the door."

Dan: "How did you know we were here? After the events of today, my plans were to shut down everything until we could clear our heads. We only stopped here to get a few things before heading home."

Jake: "It was a chance I was willing to take. Can you please open the door?"

Dan: "I'll be right there."

As Dan ends the call, he looks over at Debbie and Bob with a puzzled look on his face: "What do you make of this?"

Bob O'Reilly: "He's in charge of the shooting. Anyone with half a brain can see the possible connection with the blast. He's just being thorough. I suggest we let him in before he starts getting concerned."

With that said, Debbie heads from the office to the front door. As she opens it, she greets the two members of the task force: "I'm sorry about the delay, you caught us off guard. Please come in, Dan and Bob are in the back office."

Jake: "We understand that this is a difficult time for everyone. We won't take up too much of your time."

Before Jake and Kent's arrival, Bob brought two extra chairs into the office.

As everyone sits down, Jake wants to avoid the appearance of an interrogation by showing more concern for the Congressman than the incident. As he prepares to ask him about his present state of mind, someone else decides to speak first.

Its Dan who decides to take a proactive approach by asking the first question: "Have you heard anything about the cause of the blast?"

Jake: "I suspect its too early to know anything definitive but all indications suggest it was a car bomb, not a gas explosion. The only way a car can explode with that amount of force has to be intentional."

117

Bob O'Reilly: "I guess this being an accident is no longer on the table."

Kent: "I doubt anyone in this room thought it was an accident from the moment it occurred. Your survival instincts had to be front and center, don't you think?"

Debbie McGinnis: "The shooting was so surreal that it left us looking for answers as to how Dan could garner such hatred. Coming out against crime and terrorism are not exactly unique positions. What was the catalyst that could lead to such a violent reaction? We are still trying to figure that out."

Bob O'Reilly, turning toward Jake: "What you appear to be saying is that the shooter, failing to complete his objective in Toms River, has upped the ante. Do I have that right?"

Jake: "While we suspect that both events are connected, the motive behind the attacks remain a mystery, as is the fact that both attempts, at least on the surface, managed to miss the mark."

Dan McGinnis: "That sounds like a nice way of saying that this maniac is not that proficient at his job. I find little solace in his lack of skill. When he missed me in Toms River, he decided to blow up a neighborhood? Having failed with the bomb, what crazy method will he use next?"

Kent: "When you use terms like maniac, you run the risk of missing the point of the attacks. It's easier on you and your campaign if we are looking for an unhinged mad man with a delusional opinion of you and your bid for the Senate. It suggests that the reasons behind the attacks are not the product of rational thought. Taking that approach might be just as dangerous. It keeps everyone from looking inward."

Jake: "If we can take a step back for a moment, after yesterday's shooting and today's bombing, have you had any thoughts about your run for the Senate?"

Dan: "I'd be lying if I said otherwise. While I stand fast in my belief that I would be an asset for the citizens of New Jersey if elected to the Senate, being a martyr was never a consideration. We are still weighing our options, which I hope will stay in this room. If the press thought I was wavering, they could sink my campaign tomorrow."

Jake: "No one's looking to force your hand or pressure you into anything. Our investigations never include the press. We keep all information confidential and this case is no exception. You can make your decision on your own timetable."

Bob O'Reilly: "I don't want anyone to get the idea that we are looking for an out. Dan is the right man for the job. While we may have to modify our approach to campaigning, I doubt we will choose the other path."

Debbie: "While I may be part of his political campaign, Dan is also my husband and the father of our children. I'm not as confident as Bob in our commitment to the campaign. While I would prefer to continue, it will depend on how confident I can be in Dan's safety. I'd be lying if I said the bombing did not cast doubt about continuing the campaign."

Jake: "All of your doubts and concerns are totally understandable. I wanted to be sure how everyone felt before discussing this further."

Jake: "It is our opinion that the attempts on Dan's life is politically motivated. We do not believe that these are the actions of a madman or an unhinged zealot. We believe these attacks were planned out carefully and implemented successfully."

Dan: "I appreciate your take on this, but how can you say the attempts were successful?"

Jake: "It is our belief that both attacks were designed to frighten you rather than ending your life. While the **WHY** is still unclear, the **HOW** is fairly apparent."

Kent: "To the untrained eye, the shooter appears to have missed. The sniper rifle used suggests the shooter was proficient. The shot that injured Charlie Conroy was not that difficult of a shot. If the shooter wanted you dead, you would not be here. He had plenty of opportunities to select the right moment. He chose to send a message."

Jake: "As for the bombing, it is our opinion that it was triggered intentionally while you were near the site but not directly in harm's way. The only viable way to set off the bomb was via remote. The bomber had to position himself with a clear view of the area. He chose to set it off while you were a safe distance away."

Bob O'Reilly: "That's not in line with what the press is saying. They are reporting that the truck prevented us from getting closer to the explosion, probably saving our lives in the process."

Kent: "That requires us to believe the blast was either accidental or on a timer, neither scenario passes muster."

Jake: "If the blast came from an exploding car, which seems to be the most likely source, the strength of the blast would require the car to be loaded down with explosives. That cannot be accidental. As for the timer, there were too many delays possible to properly set a timer with any accuracy. It was ignited via a remote."

Debbie: "Well, where does that leave us?"

Jake: "We need to expose the person responsible for organizing the attacks. There is someone out there who decided that letting the election take its own course was not sufficient. In order to obtain the desired result, they needed to put their hand on the scale."

Bob O'Reilly: "This is hard to wrap my head around. We may be running against Phil Trooien but I can't fathom that anyone on his side would go to such extremes?"

Kent: "We believe this is more complicated than you realize. There are two parties in this campaign. Both parties could possibly benefit from these attacks. We cannot allow ourselves to concentrate in one direction, or we risk missing the perpetrator."

As the room falls into momentary silence, everyone is aware that Kent's remarks hit a nerve.

Where this meeting goes from here is anyone's guess but it will not include emotional outbursts or unguarded comments. All responses will be well thought out and calculated.

Being told that you are suspects in the attacks is a lot to take in. All three are looking toward Jake with a suspicious eye, requiring careful thought before speaking. If they were not concerned that calling for an attorney would place them in a difficult position with Jake Patrick, they would be on the phone right now.

Dan: "There is no way I would ever place anyone in harm's way. Running for office has its limits. Campaigns have been going on for decades, some more contentious than others."

Dan: "No one could justify such drastic action. That's not who I am nor do I believe any of my people would go to such an extreme. We will open our doors to you and your team. I'm confident you will not find your suspect in our midst."

Jake: "I'm glad you feel that way Congressman, but we are not the enemy. Whatever the reason, there's someone out there that thought it a good idea to kill dozens of Americans, either on purpose or to make a point. Right now, you appear to be the reason for the attacks."

Jake: "I've already cleared it with the governor but its important that you and your team are on board. Until further notice, Kent Baldauf will be in charge of your security. His training and expertise is a better fit for the job than your present security force, which is already down one man."

Dan: "Doesn't it feel odd to have one of the people who are investigating us be responsible for protecting us?"

Kent: "We are not investigating you, we are simply not eliminating you and your campaign from scrutiny. Anyone politically connected, in any way, remains potential suspects until we can prove otherwise. I'm sorry if that makes you uncomfortable, but we can't let anything interfere with our process."

Jake: "If you believe that your people are as innocent as you suggest, you have nothing to worry about. As for security, you have our best man by your side, which should be a welcome addition, not a burden."

Bob O'Reilly: "Where do we go from here?"

Jake: "Run your campaign as you see fit. When discussing the need to move about in public, Kent needs to be front and center in those discussions. He will arrange the security detail and suggest how and where to allow you access to the public and under what circumstances he deems it to be safe. He's not here to tell you how to do your job."

Kent: "I will start with your two security guards. Officers Warren and Leininger will be under my supervision. After preparing a strategy for moving forward, the governor has authorized me to increase the protection, if need be. I suggest you ask my opinion before booking any public venue until we have this situation under control."

Jake: "As for our investigation, I'll need you to provide me with contact information on every member of your campaign team, whether paid employees or volunteers. My team will take it from there."

Kent: "If I can make a suggestion, it would be better for everyone if Dan addresses all of his people to let them know that our investigative team requires their cooperation. We don't need a combative atmosphere when questioning them, if the need to do so arises."

Dan: "I will address them all first thing in the morning, including the introduction of Kent Baldauf to our security team. You will have the list of everyone in the morning as well. Right now, if it is okay with you, I would like some privacy to discuss the future direction of the campaign with Bob and Debbie."

Jake nods his approval as he and Kent rise to take their leave. As they exit the offices, Jake turns to Kent: "Obviously, your first priority is keeping Dan safe. Now that you have become our eyes and ears inside his campaign, we will be looking to you to notice anything that might be deemed suspicious."

Kent: "That goes without saying. My opinion of Dan places him in the innocent category. His responses appear to be genuine. I'm withholding judgment on the other two."

Jake: "Let's get back to the office. You have a busy schedule beginning tomorrow."

Thursday, May 9th
The Residence of Josef Habib
Fairfield, NJ - 7:46PM

————————————————

As Habib's team is discussing the events of the day and their plans for tomorrow, Josef is waiting for that all important phone call to come through.

He ignored the numerous calls that came his way since the bombing, primarily because he was not ready to address the attack. Now that he has met with his fellow jihadists, he's ready to talk to the benefactor, hopefully while his team is still present. Everyone needs to hear the words Josef is about to use that will change things permanently.

His plan to rid the world of Jake Patrick will begin in earnest once he brings their latest team member on board. A member that will not come willingly but an important piece of the puzzle, if they are to succeed with their jihad.

As if on cue, Habib's phone rings, revealing that the call is coming from the benefactor. He answers the call on the second ring: "I was hoping you would call this evening."

Without a second delay, the benefactor explodes in a tirade of emotion, aiming their rathe on Habib and his actions: "What the hell did you do? I've been trying to reach you all day. The bomb you chose to use today has killed dozens of innocent people, proving to me that you have no regard for human life. No one was supposed to get hurt, much less die."

Benefactor: "We are through. If I could find a way to turn you in to the authorities without incriminating myself, I would do so, but that's a risk I cannot take. I need you to

lose my number and forget you ever had any contact with me. I'm destroying this burner phone after we end this call and I suggest you do the same. I had no idea I was dealing with a maniac."

Habib: "Am I to assume you are unhappy with how I chose to frighten the Congressman? I can assure you he must be at his wit's end by now. Isn't that what you wanted me to do?"

Benefactor: "You killed people! You injured dozens more without remorse. We had a plan that you chose to ignore. I was a fool to trust you."

Habib: "I'm glad you came to your senses about contacting the authorities. I'm sure you must realize that such a threat is a two-way street. A call from me, even an anonymous one, would have them at your door in an instant. I've recorded all of our conversations, just in case you lost your nerve, which I assume is what this call is all about."

Habib: "Whether you like it or not, we are now connected at the hip. We sink or swim together. I am in control, not you. You will do what I say or you will become the target of my rathe. That can end one of two ways; with you in prison or dead."

Benefactor: "My god, you can't be serious? I'm no killer. I promise you that no one will ever know about any of this. We can go our separate ways and leave all of this behind us."

Habib: "I'm afraid that does not work for me. I have a plan that has yet to be implemented which requires you to play an integral part in its success. You have no say in the matter. Do what I ask or pay the price for your failure to do so. What you say next will determine the rest of your life. Help me achieve my directive and you can go on living without worry of exposure. Fail to assist me in any way, and your life will be over."

After a period of silence, which feels likes an eternity to Habib and his fellow extremists, the benefactor responds: "What is it you need me to do?"

Thursday, May 9th
Home of Senator Trooien
Bedminster, NJ - 8:37PM

After Howard Clarke left for the evening, Phil and Roberta Trooien try to relax, in an attempt to relieve their anxiety. The calming silence does not last very long as the Senator's cellphone rings. He can see that the call is coming from Jake Patrick.

As he looks over at Roberta, who nods approval, he answers the call: "This is Senator Trooien."

Jake: "Senator, this is Jake Patrick. We need to meet with you, first thing in the morning, if possible. We have a few questions that need answering. Do you have a campaign office where we can meet?"

Trooien: "I'm running things at of my home right now. Howard Clarke, my Chief of Staff, has an office of volunteers working out of Edison while my Senate staff helps organize things from Washington. Its best if we meet here, Jake."

Jake: "We will be there around 10:00AM. Please have Mr. Clarke in attendance as well. We will need to talk to the rest of your campaign management team at some point, preferably tomorrow. Is there anyone else that should be in attendance?"

Trooien: "The only other person overseeing things is my aide, Liz Anderson. I can arrange for her to be in attendance as well."

Jake: "That would be great. Things have been going off the rails quickly and I need to get them back on track."

Trooien: "I'll see you tomorrow morning, Jake."

As the call ends, Phil turns to Roberta: "It looks like our campaign team can no longer be considered innocent bystanders. I'm sure the bombing raised the temperature pretty high with Jake and his team. Our best course of action is to cooperate fully."

Roberta: "I'm sure he's only following protocol. You have known Jake a long time. I doubt he suspects you of anything."

Trooien: "I'm going to have to call Liz. This has to be a unified front when interacting with Jake and his team."

Roberta: "I'll call Howie. We can meet here at nine, giving us time to prepare for Jake's visit."

Whether tomorrow's meeting will make matters worse or better is anyone's guess. The one thing they know for sure is that there are more suspects than victims.

Chapter Eleven

What's Beneath the Surface?

Friday, May 10ᵗʰ
Senator Trooien's Home
Bedminster, NJ - 10:03AM

As Jake and Ava make their way toward the Senator's home, they pull to the side of the road in order to make sure they are on the same page as to how they expect the meeting to proceed.

Jake: "We are walking a fine line here. On one hand, we need their cooperation, while on the other hand, we will be letting them know that their campaign staff are suspects in the attacks. The more we can accomplish before they become aware of their status, the better."

Ava: "I doubt Senator Trooien is unaware of their inclusion on our short list of suspects. Being the opponent of the person under attack tends to make you a suspect, no matter the outcome."

Jake: "You're probably right but I still want to remain as non committal as possible before showing our hand."

Ava: "We'll be fine. Should I begin or do you want to start the discussion?"

Jake: "Since Phil is a friend, it has to be me. You can jump in anytime but I feel that I have to make the initial overture. If it turns out that the person we are looking for is a member of their team, he or she, most likely, will be in the room. This is too involved to have been orchestrated by a campaign worker or volunteer."

Ava: "We should have invited Keri Ann to accompany us. She's the best profiler I know."

Jake: "My wife could help but there would be no way to explain her involvement. The two of us will have to do."

As they pull up to the gate, they hit the entry button and the gate immediately begins to swing open. The camera must have alerted those inside since no one said anything at all.

As Jake reaches the circular driveway, he sees Roberta Trooien standing outside the front door. As she smiles, she points to the open space on the side of the house. The interview is about to begin.

———————————————————

Senator Trooien, addressing Howard Clarke and Liz Anderson: "They will be here any moment. Remember, we need to be cooperative but its better not to be too outspoken."

Phil: "We are all suspects until proven otherwise. Any overt actions or emotional outbursts will not make things better. That old saying, *'Thou protests too much'* is in play here. Just try and relax and be yourselves."

As if on cue, Roberta leads their guests into the office. Phil stands, extending his hand to Jake and Ava. He then directs them to the two open seats that have been placed for their arrival.

Roberta: "I will leave all of you alone. If you need anything, just let me know." As she leaves the room, she looks back at Phil and silently mouths the words *Good Luck*.

Phil: "Its good to see you Jake. I wish it were under different circumstances but I guess you play the hand that is dealt."

Phil: "After the events of the past few days, your need to meet with us is not unexpected. How could the opponent of the person being targeted not be on the suspect list? Whatever we can do to alleviate your concerns, we are more than willing to do."

Jake's hope of waiting until the end to address their role as suspects has been smashed to smithereens. He just needs to adapt and move on: "This early in our investigation, we cannot afford to remove anyone as suspects. As for today, we are just looking to learn as much as possible about your campaign's activities leading up to the attacks. This is a fact finding mission, not an interrogation."

Ava: "What if the attacker has something against the both of you? Maybe he started with Dan and will move on to you? Until we know more, everything remains on the table."

Howie: "I'm not sure how we can help. We were all in Washington when Dan was doing his rally in Toms River. All three of us were as surprised by the shooting as was everyone else. Since when does a political campaign, even a nasty one, turn to physical violence?"

Jake: "Until we can uncover the motive behind the shooting and the bombing, we cannot answer that question. To dismiss a political angle is not only foolish but impractical. In fact, we are more convinced than ever that these attacks were politically motivated."

Liz: "If I may, that seems to be a bit of a stretch. I have been working for years in Washington and it can get pretty intense at times. Politicians can get abusive with their rhetoric but I've never seen it turn physical. It's not in the nature of the politician."

Liz: "Here we have two attempts on a candidate's life, the last one resulting in the death of a number of innocent people who happen to be in the wrong place at the wrong time. I can't think of anyone willing to go to that extreme."

Phil: "Why are you so sure this is political? From everything I've read, the press is leaning in another direction. There are a number of crazies out there who might be motivated to act irrationally. While politics is not immune to outbursts from extremists on either side of the aisle, it usually does not elevate to this level."

Howie: "According to the media, Charlie Conroy got in the way of the shooter and ended up in the hospital. A stalled truck in the road prevented Dan's car from getting dangerously close to the bomb. Why can't it be some nut with a grudge against Dan? The attacker may have missed twice but it could be luck and circumstances that accidentally got in the way."

Ava: "We already know too much to believe these failed attempts were accidental."

Phil: "Can you share your reasoning with us?"

Jake: "I will, but you need to understand that I have no problem with the press going down the wrong path for now. What we discuss needs to remain confidential. Having the shooter thinking we are taken a wrong turn is to our benefit. I'm sure you can understand that."

Howie: "If you think we are behind the attack, how do we know you are not trying to throw us off by feeding us falsehoods? Maybe trying to see how we will react?"

Phil, showing his annoyance: "Howie, enough! This is not the time for cynicism. Let Jake explain his theories and maybe we can help in some way. We are not behind these attacks, I'm sure of it. Let him do his job."

Phil turns to Jake before continuing: "I'm sorry about that. We are all on edge over this. We will keep everything we discuss confidential, you have my word."

Jake: "It is our contention that the incidents were designed to frighten Dan, not kill him."

Jake: "The shooter had multiple opportunities to take out Dan on the podium. We have concluded that the shot was not a difficult one, even for an average shooter. He waited until there was a disturbance out front and people were moving around to take his shot. He struck Conroy in the shoulder as a warning, not by mistake. It was an intentional miss."

Ava: "As for the bombing, the theory that it was on a timer is categorically false. Too many variables to accurately place Dan's car in the proper position at the exact time of the explosion. It was detonated via remote, meaning the bomber was watching from afar. It was no accident. He intended to set it off prematurely."

Jake: "If the plan was to frighten him into doing something, what would that be? Dropping the campaign? Curtailing his campaign activities? Getting out of politics all together? Who would benefit from disrupting his campaign?"

Howie: "I assume that is where we come in. The problem is more complicated than you might suspect. We are not benefitting, he is. We were ten points ahead, which in politics is comparable to the size of the Grand Canyon. A victory by a margin of just 5% would be considered a landslide."

Howie: "After being attacked, the sympathy vote alone could bridge that 10% gap in no time. The next poll will tell us how bad it is but I can almost promise you that he is closer to us in the polls after the attacks than he was before."

Phil: "I'm afraid that Howie is correct, Jake. The reason we met with the press yesterday morning was to try and minimize the sympathy vote, not capitalize on Dan's misfortune."

Phil: "We have avoided attacking Dan during the campaign because of two things; we were leading by a lot and we agree on almost everything. To attack his talking points would be the same as attacking our own."

Liz: "We have had pressure from our base supporters to get more aggressive. They react more on emotion than we do. We have refused for good reason. Don't get in the way of your success. Any political advantage from the attacks are all on Dan's side."

Ava, turning toward Senator Trooien: "While I will not pretend to be an expert on political matters, I can see the opportunity for both parties to benefit from these attacks."

Ava: "I understand that you have a crime bill that has stalled for the moment. You even mentioned it yesterday when you addressed the press. If the attacks could get that bill

back on track, having it turned into law would trump Congressman McGinnis's claims that you are not doing enough on that front. That claim appears to be the central focus of his campaign to replace you in the Senate, unless I'm mistaken?"

Phil: "I suspect you are more politically savvy than you profess to be. I would love to have my bill pass through unimpeded, but it will take a lot more than these attacks to convince a few of my fellow politicians to act in time for this to do me any good, as far as the campaign is concerned."

Howard Clarke, showing more emotion than he expected to: "Phil Trooien has served the people of New Jersey with grace and honor for more than a decade now. They are lucky to have him representing them in Washington. I can't help but take offense at having his character and motives questioned in this way."

Jake: "We are getting off track and that benefits no one. The Senator and I have known each other a long time and I consider him a friend. Until we have some answers to a few of the questions that hang over these attacks, I can't afford to allow my personal feelings to influence the investigation. This is not personal and everyone in this room needs to try and keep the emotion out of it."

Jake: "Let's approach this from a different angle. Do any of you know of someone in your campaign circle that might be taking this run for Senate a little too personally?"

Jake: "Maybe they are so enamored with Phil that their loyalty shines brightly in everything they do. They may be a little more indignant of Dan's run for Senate, meaning that they are less willing to accept his campaign as being legitimate, preferring to consider it a form of betrayal."

Liz: "We do have a number of loyal volunteers under our wing, which is true of any campaign I've been involved in over the years. Some might take it too personal, but I doubt they would go this far."

Ava: "It's a place to start. We have requested the same soul searching from the Congressman's staff. While there are many aspects of these attacks, especially the bombing yesterday, that are especially disturbing, we feel confident that there is a political angle to them. While the person committing these acts might not be political, the person responsible for putting all of this in motion has a political reason for doing so."

Howie: "If I read you correctly, you think someone with a political motive most likely hired the person who is carrying out the attacks, much like an abused wife hiring a killer to eradicate her husband."

Jake: "Unless we find out something different, this appears to be the type of crime that requires farming out the grunt work to others. Not many people are capable of this type

of physical aggression. Having someone else carry things out is preferable to doing it yourself, especially if you do not have the stomach for it."

Phil: "Jake, you will have full access to our entire team. You have my word on that. You can coordinate all matters through Liz. She's closer to our staff and volunteer network than either myself or Howie."

Jake: "Liz, we will need a complete list of everyone involved in the campaign along with the addresses and contact information. It might be a good idea if you communicate the possibility that they may be called upon to answer a few questions. The less surprises the better."

Ava: "On another topic, there's no guarantee that Dan McGinnis is the only target. The governor has authorized us to provide you with added security until we have a better handle on things."

Phil: "What type of security? We have our own team that has been in place for a number of years now. Are you suggesting we remove them for the time being?"

Jake: "We are only providing an extra layer of security. Ava is an expert on terror tactics and is my second in command. She will oversee things beginning today. Your security team will take orders from her until we feel it's no longer necessary."

Jake: "Her most important job is to advise you as to how best to handle public spaces. While your security is fine in situations that require quick reactionary responses, Ava is better at being proactive, helping you to avoid placing yourself in situations where protection is more difficult to manage."

Howie: "Do you really think we are next on the list?"

Jake: "The purpose is to prevent an attack, not try and react to one. Dan's security team could not stop the shooting. If the bomber waited until Dan's car was closer to the bomb, things would have turned out differently."

Jake: "We need to try and keep you out of harm's way. While there are no guarantees, my team can spot potential chinks in the armor that could lead to problems. I suggest you take her advice before exposing yourself to the public for now."

Phil: "I must say, I'm having difficulty coming to grips with all of this. Added security, potential criminals under our roof, a campaign of violence rather than one of ideas. This is all too much for my brain to digest."

Ava: "If it's any consolation, we do not expect this to take very long. We will find the persons responsible and end this nightmare. As long as your team and Dan's team cooperate fully, we will solve this mystery, hopefully before anyone else gets hurt."

As Jake and Ava rise, indicating they are ready to leave, Ava turns to Howard Clarke: "I will meet up with you this afternoon around 2:00PM. Hopefully you are not planning on any public appearances before then."

Howie: "We can meet here. I'll have our security team here as well. We will cooperate fully, you have my word on that."

As Jake and Ava leave, Phil begins to drop his facade as he feels enraged by the suggestion that his team might be behind the attacks.

Phil: "This is utter nonsense. To suggest we might be involved is ludicrous. I'm a respected United States Senator who was leading in the polls. By all accounts, we have nothing to fear from Dan and his campaign. Now we have to let someone from the task force decide who we see and how we approach the campaign? When this is over, I will not forget the lack of respect Jake Patrick has shown for me and my office."

As Phil is ranting away, Roberta enters the room carrying a pot of tea and four cups: "I suggest we all relax for a moment and let cooler heads prevail."

Phil: "Roberta, you're not taking Jake's side in this?"

Roberta: "Of course not, Phil. There's only one side that matters but we need to present a facade of cooperation. To do anything else would be problematic."

Roberta: "I'm still angry with the Congressman for launching his campaign against you. After all the good you have done for the state of New Jersey, he decides to challenge you by making up facts and painting you as a DO NOTHING Senator, all lies and untruths, which are the hallmark of a sleazy campaign."

Roberta: "We must be the ones to take the high road here. We cannot let any of them see how their actions have rattled our emotions. How we decide to address these attacks after we win re-election is another matter. For now, we must cooperate."

Liz: "We have nothing to hide. I'll give Jake everything he asked for and more. I'm sure none of our people are behind these attacks."

Howie: "We'll play along with this charade for now. If there is any chance that we are also in the crosshairs, the last thing I want to do is put Phil in danger."

Phil: "Liz, You need to provide me with everything that you plan on passing on to Jake. I want to be briefed before you tell him anything. If you find something that might be worth pursuing,

I want first crack at the data. I will not be blindsided by Jake Patrick, the governor or anyone else."

Roberta: "I think we are all on the same page here. We control our participation in the investigation and with that control comes options. We need to remain in charge."

Roberta: "Now with that said, let's all have a relaxing cup of tea. Everything looks better after a cup of tea."

Friday, May 10th
Inside Jake's car
Heading Back to Morristown, NJ - 11:32AM

As Jake and Ava are heading back to their office, they are discussing the recently concluded interview with Senator Trooien and his management team. Jake has learned early on that instinctual opinions are freshest immediately after the dialogue has ended.

Jake: "If I had to guess, Liz Anderson does not appear to be involved. Her demeanor appears to be genuine and she never allowed herself to get flustered, no matter how tempestuous the conversation became."

Ava: "I'm not sure that I would give her a pass just yet. While emotions were more in play from Howard Clarke and the Senator, anyone involved would have been better prepared for the questions and more in control of their reactions."

Jake: "I guess I can understand how you came to that conclusion. I attach greater weight to my instincts, which is the reason I found her to be credible. She will remain on the list until we begin to fill in the missing pieces."

Ava: "Howard Clarke wore his emotions on his sleeve. While he tried to tamper them down, his face and his body language prevented him from doing so. He took the possibility of someone in their campaign being involved personally, either because he believed it or to make us believe it."

Jake: "While Phil Trooien had more control of his emotions, he was bubbling up inside with rage. I know him a little better and his body language did not match his words. My instincts tell me he was insulted by our insinuations and that suggests that he considered himself above all of this."

Ava: "I agree, the Senator was the most upset with us. That could go both ways. Being accused of playing a part in the attacks was so outrageous or because we hit a nerve that he did not expect us to tweak."

As they continue to discuss the recent meeting, Jake's phone rings, showing the incoming caller to be Tricia Highland: "We are heading back to the office. We should be there in the next thirty minutes or so."

Tricia: "I guess it can wait until you get here."

Ava: "Now that we know you have something of interest to report, how can we wait that long? How about giving us the highlights?"

Tricia: "The terror angle is alive and well. While Gary and I were digging into our store owner in greater detail, guess what we found in Abdul Farouk's background check?"

Jake: "If I had to guess I would suspect that you were able to connect him to one of the known terror organizations that are on our radar."

Tricia: "While that would have been great, it did not happen. We did, however, find something more directly tied to the attacks. It appears that among Abdul's frequent contacts is none other than our truck driver, Mohammed Sarif. The odds of that happening has to be remote, don't you think?"

Jake: "Now we are getting somewhere. We now have two suspects to look into that might lead us where we need to go. It's going to be harder for them to hide their association now that both of them our on our radar."

Ava: "Every known associate of the two needs to be contacted and investigated. We may have an entire terror cell we knew nothing about until now."

Jake: "Start digging into our truck driver right away. We will be there shortly." As the call ends, Jake and Ava have a renewed sense of purpose. Pieces of the puzzle are starting to fall into place.

With the terror angle becoming more viable by the day, why would a political operative hire a terrorist to act as their protagonist? Was it by choice or just bad luck? Either way, they need to find both participants before someone else loses their life.

Chapter Twelve

Its Time to Pay the Piper

Friday, May 10ᵗʰ
Josef Habib's Residence
Fairfield, NJ - 1:27PM

Habib is on the phone with Mohammed Sarif after having received a call from the benefactor: "It appears that Jake Patrick will be conducting an interview this afternoon at 3:30PM in Wayne, NJ. I have the address and I'm going to arrange a warm welcome for his arrival."

Habib: "According to our source, he should be driving a late model black Chevy Traverse with the NJ license plate number S5KL3. We have our window of opportunity and I intend to capitalize on it."

Sarif: "Is there anything you need me to do?"

Habib: "You told me your company has a fleet of small vans for lighter deliveries. Can you secure one of them?"

Sarif: "Following the bombing, the authorities have seized my truck as evidence. I'm actually using one of the vans right now. What is it you need?"

Habib: "According to the local street map, the person Jake Patrick will be interviewing lives on a one way street in Wayne. We need to position the van in such a way as to have the rear door facing in the direction he will be traveling. As to my plan, it will become clear when we get together."

Sarif: "I can pick you up in 15 minutes, if that is okay?"

Habib: "I'll be ready."

Friday, May 10th
Vernon Ave.
Wayne, NJ - 3:26PM

_____

From his position in the back of the van, Habib has a clear view of Vernon Avenue through the window pane on the van's rear door. Using a pair of binoculars, he carefully scrutinizes every car coming in his direction.

The home in question is located in the center of the block. There are a few open spaces near the apartment, which should allow Jake's car to come closer to his final destination before deciding on a place to park.

As the anticipated time for his arrival draws near, Habib notices a black SUV making the turn on to the street at the far end of the block. It appears to be a black Chevy.

Almost instantaneously, he gets a ping on his phone from Alaina Assis, who is positioned near the corner as a lookout. She confirms that its Jake Patrick's car.

As Jake's car slowly makes its way down the street, without any warning, the rear doors of the van swing open as Habib points a rocket launcher at the oncoming car.

Within seconds, he fires, hitting the car just below the hood, as the rocket explodes on contact.

The force of the blast lifts the car skyward as it bursts into flames. The force of the blast is so strong that it sends the car spinning in the air, finally ending upside down on the ground, crushing the soft hood downward into the car's interior, trapping anyone still alive inside the burning vehicle.

As the effects of the blast continue to shoot toward the sky, Habib closes the rear doors and the van takes off, leaving the chaos behind.

Josef Habib has accomplished what many others in the past were unable to do, rid the world of its most despised infidel, Jake Patrick.

Friday, May 10th
Wayne General Hospital
Wayne, NJ - 5:12PM

––––––––––––––––––––––––

As the remaining members of the New Jersey Special Projects Task Force gather at the hospital, the shock is beginning to set in. One of their own is in surgery and the outcome is tenuous, at best.

Tricia: "How could this have happened? Someone was waiting for him to arrive for the interview. This must have been a setup from the beginning."

Kent: "The hell with diplomacy. The gloves are off on this one. Everyone responsible for this will pay."

Ava: "Political operatives do not send rockets into oncoming cars. We suspected a terror connection and this confirms it. Why a political operative would hire a terrorist to carry out their agenda is anyone's guess."

Tricia: "Someone needed to provide the radicals with detailed information about today's interview in Wayne. Who else knew about the interview, including the when and where?"

Ava: "The suspect was aware. He agreed to the appointment. I'm sure he communicated with others as to the reason behind the interview. I know if I was contacted about this, my next call would be to my superiors as to why this was happening and how I should handle it."

At that moment, a doctor makes his way into the waiting room, removing his surgical mask as he prepares to discuss the matter: "He's resting comfortably for the moment but he is far from okay. He has some serious burns and his shoulder was badly dislocated. My main concern, however, has to do with head trauma. The concussion from the blast was severe. There was some bleeding and a significant amount of swelling. We have him in a medically induced coma for now while we monitor his vitals."

Doctor: "How he managed to pull himself out of the car and away from the vehicle is anyone's guess but it saved his life, at least for the moment. Until the swelling subsides and we can better determine his true condition, we cannot rule out anything."

Doctor: "I suggest you all go home for now. It will be hours before we can even consider trying to return him to consciousness."

As the doctor leaves, the team turns their attention toward the far corner of the waiting room. As they make their way toward Jake, he remains lost in thought, unaware of what's happening around him. He has remained by himself since they arrived at the hospital. Knowing Jake as well as they do, it's obvious that he is blaming himself for Gary's condition.

Ava, touching Jake on the shoulder to get his attention: "The doctor says that Gary is doing as well as can be expected. They have him in a medically induced coma that will probably keep him sedated until tomorrow. There's nothing else for us to do here so we should head back to the office."

Jake, without making eye contact with anyone: "He's here because of me. If I wasn't waiting for the governor's call, it would have been me in the car. Gary volunteered to take my place. He should be out here with you."

Kent: "That's a game of **WHAT IF** that is not helping anyone right now. The people responsible for what happened are not in this room. Whoever they are, they signed their own death warrant today, if I have any say in the matter."

Tricia: "The best thing we can do right now is find these bastards. We have some clues that we can pursue that center on the store owner and the trucker. I'm sure Gary would rather have us looking for them rather than sitting here."

Tricia, reaching gently toward Jake: "Jake, we need to go."

Jake rises from his seat and begins waging a war between his emotions and his warrior self. As he comes to grips with how best to proceed, he turns toward his team: "We have a lot to do and little time to do it."

Jake: "I need Tricia and Kent to handle the terror angle. My first call will be to Governor James to begin opening every door in the city of Wayne to the both of you. The first order of business is to monitor every street camera in the area for clues as to who is responsible. You do not blow a hole in a street without someone noticing."

Jake: "Ava and I will stay in the political arena. The person ultimately responsible for this is part of that select network of people that swear their loyalty to the constitution while, in reality, they tend to be more self serving than they are servants of the people."

Jake, looking more determined than ever: "Nothing is off the table. Whatever means are necessary to find the people responsible is fair game."

Kent: "That's all I needed to hear, boss."

As the team leaves the hospital, the expressions on their faces say volumes. The people responsible will now have to deal with an investigative team that, not only are

looking for them, but have a personal score to settle, not an enviable position for them to be in.

Before reaching their cars, Jake has the governor on the phone: "Governor James, we are going to need your help."

Friday, May 10th
Farouk's Religious Artifacts
Paterson, NJ - 5:57PM

_____

As Abdul locks the front door, placing the closed sign prominently for all to see, he heads to the back room where Josef Habib is waiting for him. As he sits down, the expression on his face is one of confusion and concern.

Abdul: "How could this happen? According to the news, a member of the task force is presently in the hospital fighting for his life. The person in the car appears to have been Gary Ceepo, not Jake Patrick. What could have gone wrong? Were you given incorrect information?"

Josef: "Our benefactor is so frightened right now, there is no way we were fed false information. Somehow, Jake Patrick must have had a change in plans. There's no one to blame here except for unforeseen circumstances."

Josef: "The problem for all of us going forward is that we have woken the sleeping bear. Jake Patrick and his team will be using all of their resources to find us and they are not without resources."

Abdul: "I fear that was our best chance to get to Jake Patrick. It will not be any easier going forward. Maybe we need to blend back into oblivion for the time being until things quiet down."

Josef: "That is not longer an option. Once BAHRUN activates one of their cells, there is no turning back. We complete our mission or we die in the attempt."

Abdul: "Then where do we go from here?"

Josef: "It appears that our benefactor is still unknown to the authorities. That gives us an advantage regarding intel."

Josef: "What I need to do is place the benefactor on notice that being exposed as a criminal is not the only problem they need to consider. We are going to up the ante, as the benefactor's life is now the cost of failure."

Abdul: "Josef, can you be sure you got away clean? An explosion of that magnitude should have drawn a number of eyes."

Josef: "We pulled away in seconds. Anyone nearby would be drawn to the explosion itself. We blended into traffic too quickly to be noticed, I'm sure of it."

Abdul: "Time will not be on our side from this point forward."

Josef: "We have no choice but to succeed. When we learn where Jake Patrick will be heading tomorrow, we need to end this, once and for all."

Josef: "BAHRUN has provided us with four new passports to use when the job is done. They indicate that we are German citizens. I've booked us on a flight from Philadelphia to Berlin, leaving on Sunday evening. Our time in America is over."

Abdul: "Does that give us enough time?"

Josef: "It has to be enough time. We have to end this tomorrow."

Friday, May 10th
Office of the NJ Special Projects Task Force
Morristown, NJ - 6:12PM

―――――――――――――

Jake: "Lets get down to business. Does anyone doubt the connection between the attacks on the Congressman and the rocket that nearly killed Gary?"

As Jake looks around the room, words are not necessary as everyone nods their approval: "All of this started on the political side, requiring someone else to carry out the actual attacks. I suspect that the person hired to do so turned out to be a terrorist, not just a hired gun. While I have my doubts that our political suspect knew of the radical nature of the attacker, none of that matters right now."

Jake: "Okay, let's take stock of what we already know. What do we know that might help us to move forward?"

Tricia Highland is the first to speak: "We know that our two terror suspects, Abdul Farouk and Mohammed Sarif, know each other and have communicated on numerous occasions. That cannot be by chance. They are both involved in the attacks in some way."

Kent: "While we can't tie Abdul directly to any of the attacks, Mohammed Sarif is front and center on the car bombing. It's obvious that he was there to prevent the Congressman's car from getting too close to the bomb."

Ava: "We have Homeland Security cross referencing all available data on the two suspects, hoping to find additional links that might expose other potential co-conspirators."

Ava: "From what we have learned about these two so far, neither one appears to be anything more than foot soldiers. There are others out there, including someone who is in charge and responsible for the attacks."

Jake: "The governor has the City of Wayne working overtime examining every camera in the vicinity of the rocket attack to find those responsible. I hope to have their data in the next few hours."

Jake: "I asked the Governor to request the same security footage from the previous attacks. If we get lucky, we may be able to come away with a number of suspects, including the person who placed the car bomb on the street. As for the attack on Gary, finding the person who launched the rocket is priority number one."

Kent: "Once we identify potential suspects, I suggest we contact Bill Gregor at the regional FBI office. Their facial recognition software is **State of the Art**."

Jake: "Kent, I'll leave it to you to get Bill Gregor on board. Once we have the footage from all three attacks, we can forward key footage to him in the morning for analysis."

Ava, turning to Jake: "Could it be possible that the person who hired the terrorist knew what they were getting themselves into?"

Jake: "I doubt it. I can't logically link the two together in my mind. Sometimes the best answer is the simplest answer. They managed to hire the wrong person for the job."

Jake: "If I'm right, our political antagonist must be beside themselves with fear over the results of their actions. With any luck, it may be too much to bear and they will come forward before more people get hurt or killed, politics be damned."

Kent: "While that would be great, I'm not expecting to get that lucky. Every time a jihadist uses a non-believer to assist them in their act of terror, the threats of personal bodily harm to every person in their family usually follows that request. I doubt we will get an assist on that front."

Tricia: "I'm afraid Kent is right."

Jake: "Speaking of politics, does anyone have a theory as to who might be involved?"

Ava: "Unfortunately, nothing that might point us in the right direction. Both campaigns remain suspect. While there are just a handful of management on both sides, there are

dozens of campaign workers who need to be looked into, though time is not on our side for all we need to accomplish."

Kent: "What about the volunteer Gary was hoping to interview? He was a member of the Trooien team that had posted a number of social media comments condemning Congressman McGinnis for his false accusations against Senator Trooien on crime. His passion for the Senator was the reason he wound up first on our list of people to interview."

Ava: "He also knew the exact time and place of the interview, which could have led to the attack. We have to talk to him first thing in the morning."

Jake: "Unfortunately, my instincts tell me he's the least likely suspect."

Tricia: "How so?"

Jake: "Prior to the interview, we informed the Trooien campaign that I was going to interview one of their volunteers who posted some fairly aggressive material on line. We all agree that the rocket attack was intended for me, not Gary. I was supposed to be in that car."

Jake: "The only person who knew I was not going to be there was the volunteer. I felt it the proper thing to do to call him prior to Gary's arrival, informing him that I would not be conducting the interview. If he was involved, that change in plans would have triggered a phone call. The jihadist responsible did not get the message or the attack would have been called off."

Kent: "Just to be sure, I would like to conduct an early morning interview with him anyway, if for no other reason than to determine if he told anyone else that you were not coming to see him."

Jake: "Call him this evening and arrange for him to meet with us here at the office. No more home visits until we find our radical jihadist."

Jake: "Since we have few clues to work with, its time we fall back on our experience. What does our common sense gene tell us about who is more likely to be behind these attacks?"

Tricia: "If I had to pick a side, any advantage appears to be on the side of the McGinnis campaign. While the death and injuries associated with the two attacks on the Congressman does not fall under the purview of either campaign, Dan's the beneficiary of the attacks."

Ava: "I have to agree with Tricia. I suspect that whomever is responsible, the plan was to frighten, not injure. It was the hired gun who decided that casualties were an acceptable outcome of the attacks."

Kent: "If I'm being true to myself, I have to agree that Dan benefits the most. Both campaigns are too savvy not to see how these attacks might play out."

Kent: "Phil Trooien and Howard Clarke said as much immediately after the first attack. The sympathy vote can be extremely powerful. If the Senator's campaign is behind this, why make things harder than they need to be?"

Jake: "There's one fly in the ointment, so to speak. While we contacted the Trooien team about today's interview with one of their volunteers, we never mentioned that to the McGinnis team. If they are behind this, how did the terrorists learn about the time and place?"

Kent: "I'm afraid it may have been me. When the text came in about the interview, I was with the McGinnis team. I mentioned it to them as a precursor to the fact that we may also be interviewing some of their campaign staff shortly. I never thought that it could lead to an attempt on Jake's life."

Jake: "No one could have predicted that such an insignificant event could lead to such tragedy. Unfortunately, it leaves us with both campaigns remaining as potential suspects."

Kent: "Maybe its time we set a trap. Provide different information to each party and see if anyone bites?"

As they discuss options, Jake's phone pings: "It appears we have all of our surveillance videos arriving to our office mainframe. There are a few highlighted sections that need to be analyzed first but the rest is raw footage from the pre-determined timeframes requested."

Jake: "It's going to be long night for me. There's no chance of me sleeping until we get some answers. The three of you need to get some rest and be ready to attack the problem in the morning."

Ava: "I'm afraid you are not doing this alone. I suspect that there will be four sets of eyes working through the night. We have one of ours fighting for his life in the hospital. There is no higher priority for any of us than finding those responsible."

Kent: "I don't know about the rest of you but I'm ordering dinner before anything else."

As the rest of the team prepares themselves for a long night, there's another team looking to finalize their mission before the sun sets tomorrow.

Friday, May 10th
Habib Residence
Fairfield, NJ - 8:22PM

————————————————

As the BAHRUN terror cell gathers for that all important phone call, Josef Habib is planning how best to stress the urgency of tomorrow's much needed intelligence to the benefactor.

Josef: "Time is no longer on our side. We cannot wait for another opportunity to present itself. We have to know where Jake Patrick will be tomorrow, not in a few days."

Alaina: "That can be difficult for the benefactor to accomplish unless we get lucky. I doubt that Jake Patrick is sharing his hourly schedule with everyone. How does the benefactor find what we need without creating suspicion?"

Josef: "That is not our problem."

As if on cue, the call Habib expects is now coming in. As he answers the call, he does not wait for a verbal response on the other end: "The timetable has changed, We have less than 24 hours to complete our mission. I must know where Jake Patrick will be tomorrow. You have until noon to provide me with that location."

After what appears to be an eternity of silence, the benefactor responds: "I'm afraid your failed attempt earlier in the day has left me in the dark."

Benefactor: "Jake Patrick and his team have closed ranks and notified both campaigns that they must cancel all events until further notice. Neither campaign has a direct connection to his team anymore. We have no way of keeping track of his movements. I'm afraid you had your chance and you came away empty."

Habib, allowing his rage to reach the surface: "I'm afraid that is your problem not mine. If I don't get the information I need, you and your family will have bigger problems than anything Jake Patrick is dealing with at the moment. How you get it is up to you. Not getting it is no longer an option. I hope we understand each other."

Benefactor: "You leave my family out of this. I will find a way to get you what you want. If I fail, you can do what you want with me."

Josef: "How brave of you to offer yourself in place of your family. This is not our first time dealing with infidels who are willing to protect their families at all costs. You have until noon. After that, I suggest you spend your time looking over your shoulder because my people will be coming for you AND your family. Your request is denied."

As Habib hangs up the phone, his team appears to be less confident that the benefactor will perform under stressful conditions.

Josef, trying to project confidence: "We will have the information we need. Everyone will gather here in the morning, prepared to carry out our mission. Only bring what is truly necessary with you. You will not be returning home. From this point forward, our present lives in America will no longer exist."

Chapter Thirteen

Now Its Personal

Saturday, May 11th
Office of The NJ Special Projects Task Force
Morristown, NJ - 6:27AM

After a long evening of looking at videos from a hundred different angles, they have uncovered a few of the missing pieces that offer a clearer picture of those involved in the attacks. For example, the team was able to confirm the participation of both Abdul Farouk and Mohammed Sarif.

Abdul was driving the car that contained the explosives. He parked it on the block hours before the arrival of the Congressman's car. He was also seen on one of the street cameras in the area just before the car exploded, leaving little doubt that he was the person who triggered the blast.

As for Mohammed Sarif, no one needed camera footage to see his involvement with the car bomb. He was front and center when his truck stalled in the road. However, it appears he played an important part in the rocket attack, as well.

He drives for a delivery company called **Same Day Delivery**. The name was plastered all over his truck, near where the bomb exploded. A street camera also caught a view of a small delivery van with the same name at the site of the rocket attack that injured Gary Ceepo. While the camera did not actually capture the rocket launch, the van left the area immediately following the blast, indicating to the team that the person responsible for launching the rocket was, most likely, inside the van.

A third possible suspect was flagged by Homeland Security from a street camera just south of the rocket attack. They found a female acting suspiciously a block away. She was standing around, with no apparent purpose, observing the traffic that was turning on to Vernon Ave.

When Gary turned on to the street, she immediately took out her phone and sent what appeared to be a text message. It could have been a signal of some kind. While they

could not get a clear shot of her face, they were convinced she was acting as a lookout, waiting for Gary to arrive at the scene.

After the explosion, the street cameras were able to follow her a few blocks to a Nissan Altima sedan. As she made a u-turn on the two lane road, driving away from the scene, they were able to get a view of her license plate number.

The car is registered to a fitness franchise by the name of **F45 Training Fitness**, one of many in the state. They expect to have the name of the person assigned to that car no later than this morning.

After examining hours of raw video footage, Jake's team could not find anyone that was worth a second look, other than the three already identified.

As for the cameras surrounding the Toms River shooting, the footage came way with no red flags. If the three suspects were in the area, none were caught on camera. They lost a golden opportunity of seeing the shooter on video when it was determined that no cameras pointed at the entry to the building at 621 West St.

Jake, addressing the rest of his team, all showing signs of exhaustion from a long and arduous night: "When I received the videos last evening, I called Madeline Hampton to ask for her help. She agreed to have her entire team assist us in our efforts. They promised to be here around eight this morning."

Tricia: "That was a smart move, Jake. While we could've used local law enforcement to surveil the radicals, trained agents make better spies; less chance of being discovered."

Kent: "That takes care of the surveillance. How should we proceed on the political front?"

Jake: "Yesterday, Kent made a suggestion, one that might be worth pursuing. Each of the campaign management teams will be told a different story as to my schedule for the day. If our instincts are correct, the info will make its way to the terror cell. We just have to see which location becomes the right one."

Ava: "We told both teams that they had to suspend their campaigns until further notice. Approaching them now with intel seems to be a bit of a stretch, does it not?"

Jake: "While I happen to agree with you, we do have a card to play that might appear to be less suspicious."

Jake: "Kent was supposed to remain with the McGinnis campaign until we captured the suspect. Ava was assigned the same responsibilities with the Trooien campaign."

Jake: "It seems logical for us to provide them with clarification as to why we requested them to stand down. That would give us an opportunity to work my schedule into the conversation."

Tricia: "I can see that working. The hard part will be using Jake, or whoever pretends to be Jake, as a target. We already have guns, bombs and rockets being used as weapons. Can we keep our target safe?"

Jake: "I'm counting on our surveillance teams following the three jihadists to a central location, one that exposes the rest of their terror cell. We may be able to end this without having to worry about defending either location."

As they continue their discussion, Ava's phone rings. The call indicates that it is coming from Homeland Security: "Maybe they were able to identify the third suspect?"

As Ava steps away from the rest of the team to take the call, Tricia continues the discussion: "I hope Jake's right. We have to find a way to prevent the attack, not defend against it."

As Ava returns, her face suggests she can fill in a few of the missing pieces.

Ava: "The car was assigned to Alaina Assis, the manager of the fitness center located in Paterson, NJ. Her photo matches the body type of the suspect. We have her address and the address of the fitness center. A deep dive into her past and her social history is now a priority for the Feds."

Jake: "Okay, we have the necessary intel to track all three of our suspects. As soon as Maddy and her team arrive, we will get them into the field. Let's see if we can reach out to our two candidates. I'd like Ava and Kent to meet with them as soon as possible."

Ava: "I suggest we wait until Maddy's team arrives. Calling too early would indicate a sense of urgency that should not be there. We can't take the chance of raising anyone's suspicions."

Jake: "Okay, I can live with that. Now what we need to do is decide on the two locations to feed to the campaigns. The locations have to be logical and credible, while providing us enough security for our assault teams to remain hidden from view."

As they discuss how best to proceed, everyone is well aware that they are heading toward a conclusion, one with significant danger attached.

Saturday, May 11th
Josef Habib's Residence
Fairfield, NJ - 7:22AM

———————————————————

As Habib, Assis, Farouk and Sarif are having breakfast, everyone is exhibiting a level of anxiety commensurate with the task that lies before them. Their lives are being turned upside down and the years they have spent in America are coming to an end.

Josef: "I hope everyone followed my orders to the letter. Everything from your past that could tie directly to you needs to be placed in your rearview mirror. From this moment on, all of you are ghosts, spirits that will commit one last act of violence before disappearing into the wind."

Josef: "When the day is done, all of us will fade into oblivion as we leave this country of infidels behind, licking their wounds one last time. BAHRUN will be proud of all of us and they will forever speak our names with pride and respect."

Farouk: "We did as you asked. We have nowhere to go from here. If the benefactor does not come through, we may have to leave without accomplishing our mission."

Josef Habib: "That is not acceptable. There will be no safe place for us to go if we fail in our mission."

Josef: "I have a backup plan in place that none of you were aware of, hopefully, we do not need it."

Josef: "There's a young loyalist that I have been grooming for months now who wanted to be part of our assault on the infidels. At this moment, he has positioned himself outside of the task force office in Morristown."

Josef: "If we do not get the intel we require, we are going to conduct an assault that will take the entire building down, with Jake Patrick inside. The risk to our personal well being may be high but the cause is righteous."

Josef: "But for now, let's not give up on the benefactor just yet. For the time being, just try and relax and enjoy your breakfast."

Saturday, May 11th
Office of the NJ Special Projects Task Force
Morristown, NJ 8:42AM

————————————————

The New York City Anti-Terror Team, led by Madeline Hampton, is just arriving at Jake's office.

The team of Dennis McCollum, Mark Moorhead, Billy MacDonald, Mary Ellen Tremblay and Director Madeline Hampton have worked together with Jake's team on numerous occasions. Their combined talents have proven to be formidable.

Maddy:"I was surprised by the traffic for a Saturday morning. I expected to be here long before now. I'm sorry for the delay, Jake."

Jake: "I'm just happy to have your help. We have three suspects that we believe are part of a terror cell, acting as hitmen for a political operative. We believe the political motive behind the attacks were designed to frighten, not kill, but it appears that the terror cell had other ideas."

Maddy: "Do you have a handle on the person responsible from the political side?"

Jake: "Not yet but we are working on it. Kent Baldauf and Ava Matthews are meeting with the management teams of both campaigns shortly, hoping to feed them different information as to my whereabouts this afternoon. If we get lucky, we expect to narrow the search down to just one of the candidate's staff."

Dennis McCollum: "If I understand your objective, you must suspect the terror cell of targeting you specifically."

Jake: "The rocket attack yesterday that put Gary Ceepo in the hospital was meant for me. I was supposed to be conducting that interview, not Gary. He also took my car, which reinforced their supposition that I was the driver."

Mark Morehead: "It seems like an odd set of circumstances, having a political operative tied to a terror cell. What possibly could be the connection?"

Jake: "We think it was accidental on the part of the person doing the hiring. Somehow they were put in touch with each other and the contract was finalized. It's quite possible that the terror cell took the job in order to gain access to me."

Mary Ellen Tremblay: "Do you think this terror cell is connected to BAHRUN? They have tried to end your life in the past."

Jake: "Whoever they are, they are determined not to let anyone get in the way of their plans. They went from a single shot at the rally to a car bomb with dozens of casualties."

Jake: "Launching a rocket into a residential neighborhood could have resulted in significant collateral damage. Fortunately, the public was spared by what best can be described as the grace of God."

Maddy: "That reminds me, I should have led with this. How is Gary doing?"

Jake: "We are still waiting for a call from the hospital. They put him in a medically induced coma as they wait for the swelling in his brain to subside enough to better evaluate his condition."

Dennis: "It goes without saying that all of us have Gary in our prayers. As for today, what is it you need us to do?"

Jake: "We have the home addresses for all three suspects, along with their employment data. I'd like to divide everyone into groups of two with Tricia Highland being your sixth person. We have three suspects to follow who could lead us to the rest of their terror cell, including the all important leader making the decisions."

Jake: "Once our head jihadist learns my schedule for the day, a phone call should follow, requiring his team to get together. They might just lead us to a place where we can end this mess without firing a shot."

Maddy: "Mark and I will handle the truck driver, Mohammed Sarif. Mary Ellen and Dennis can take the store owner, Abdul Farouk. That leaves Billy and Tricia to watch the fitness manager, Alaina Assis."

Billy: "What if they have already left for work?"

Jake: "I will contact all three businesses around nine thirty. If I track them down at work, you can modify your surveillance. Everyone lives close by so changing locations can be accomplished in minutes, if necessary."

Jake: "The important thing is to be prepared when the call comes through."

Jake: "Both Kent and Ava will be meeting with the campaign people in the next half hour or so. After they leave, I suspect our mystery person will make the call that will let the jihadists know where they can find me later in the day."

Jake, handing files to each of the surveillance teams: "Here's all the info we have on the suspects, including photos. If you leave now, you should be in place before that call is made. Whatever you do, please do not lose them."

As everyone leaves the office, Jake is alone with his thoughts. He wants to call the hospital but thinks better of it. The doctors promised to reach out to him when they have something to report.

He decides to pass the time reviewing the video files that have kept him up all evening. Maybe, after having his morning coffee, he can see something of value this he failed to see the first time. At least it will keep him busy until he hears from Kent and Ava.

Saturday, May 11th
McGinnis Campaign Headquarters
Middletown, NJ - 9:20AM

As Kent Baldauf pulls up to the Congressman's headquarters, he can see that priorities have changed in a few short days. There are four security personnel stationed outside the office, two near the entrance door and two patrolling the street a few hundreds yards away.

Kent smiles to himself as he sees that Dan McGinnis took his suggestions to heart. If he followed his advice to the letter, there will be a fifth member of his security team positioned inside the front door, the last wall of defense.

As Kent approaches the office, the guards recognize him immediately. One of them announces his arrival on his walkie talkie as he reaches for the door handle to let Kent in. As he enters the front bullpen area, the fifth member of the security team smiles in his direction, pointing him toward the back offices.

As Kent reaches the Congressman's office, all of Dan's key personnel are standing, awaiting his arrival. Inside the office, in addition to the Congressman, is Robert O'Reilly and Dan's wife, Debbie.

Dan: "I'm a little surprised that you called for this meeting, Kent. We have already placed our campaign on hold and, as you can see, we took your security suggestions to heart. After the rocket attack yesterday that injured one of your team members, I understand the need for you to put your attentions elsewhere for the time being."

Kent: "Jake felt that, under the circumstances, we needed to provide a lot more context concerning our decision. After all, you are running for the Senate. We did not want our motives left unclear."

O'Reilly: "There was no need for you to update us. As for the rocket attack, I can't deny that we are somewhat confused as to how that is tied to the attacks on Dan?"

Debbie: "I must admit that I had similar thoughts. I'm sure your team has a number of enemies on the terror front. Why is this attack different? If they are connected, why go from Dan to one of your team members? You must have thought the same at some point."

Kent: "I can't deny that we considered every angle, including the possibility of it having no connection at all, but we have to consider all options until matters become clearer."

Dan: "So what is it you wanted us to know?"

Kent: "We believe that the terror cell is not after Dan but after us. We think they used your campaign as a catalyst to draw us out into the open. The terror clues they left behind at the shooting were too obvious and too easy to decipher."

Kent: "Once the possibility of terror presented itself, the governor would have no choice but to have our team placed in charge of the investigation. It would help the terrorists with their plans if our attention was directed toward a political motive."

Dan: "Are you saying we were nothing but decoys?"

Kent: "That's the present theory. While it is our opinion that both campaigns are no longer suspects, we need everyone to keep their eyes open and their ears close to the ground."

Kent: "if there is even the slightest chance that using Dan as a decoy was not totally random, we're asking you to do a deep dive into all of your campaign workers, including volunteers."

Debbie: "I'm not sure how we can help? You have all of our staffs' contacts and personal data. Your team must be better at noticing inconsistencies."

Kent: "That might be true but you have something we don't have, a personal relationship with everyone. It's rare that anyone can hide their true feelings for any length of time. Those details will not show up in raw data."

Dan: "We will look into our people for you. I must say that being used as a decoy does nothing to put me at ease. Until you end this nightmare, consider me to be an asset. Whatever you need, just ask."

Kent: "That's what I wanted to hear, Congressman. We have some leads to follow and a plan in place to try and end this.

We plan on keeping you advised of what we are planning and asking you to help us by communicating to the public the belief that you remain the primary target of the attackers. The last thing we need to do is let them know we are on to them."

Kent: "With that said, here's where we share critical information about our plans moving forward. While you may no longer be suspects, we will need your help if we are to end this nightmare, once and for all."

Chapter Fourteen

Setting Everything Into Motion

Saturday, May 11th
The Home of Senator Phil Trooien
Bedminster, NJ - 9:18AM

Ava can only smile as she approaches the gate to the Senator's home. It looks a little different since her last visit. The place is overflowing with security personnel, including an armed officer near the gate entrance.

As she pulls up to the gate, the guard asks to see her ID before allowing her to enter. As he studies the photo on the card, carefully examining the person in front of him, he nods his head and makes the call.

As Ava prepares to enter the home, there's another guard protecting the entry. Standing next to the guard is Roberta Trooien, waiting to escort her in.

Roberta: "Its good to see you again Ms. Matthews. I suspect Mr. Patrick is busy with other matters today."

Ava: "Jake has a lot on his plate. I'm afraid you're stuck with me. If you would be so kind as to point me in the right direction?"

Roberta: "I'll do better than that, I'll take you there. Phil is waiting for you in his office."

As Ava enters the office, she is greeted by Howard Clarke and Liz Anderson, along with the Senator. Ava's relieved to have the entire management team present for the meeting.

Ava: "Senator Trooien, I appreciate you seeing me today."

Phil: "Please, I'd prefer you call me Phil. We have suspended our campaign for the time being, as you suggested. With everything that has occurred, It was not an unreasonable request. I'm not sure why you felt we needed to meet today?"

Ava: "Jake wanted me to clear a few things up for you, if that is okay? Having you take a pause in an important campaign was not an easy ask. We just wanted you to know why we made the request."

Howard Clarke: "As Phil has already intimated, we thought it was obvious. There's a mad man out there targeting politicians."

Ava: "That's part of why I'm here today. There's been some changes in our thought process."

Ava: "We no longer think that there's a political angle to any of this. It is our opinion that a terror cell targeted Dan McGinnis in order to come up with a reason for getting our team put in charge of the investigation. The clues left behind at the shooting in Toms River suggests a terror connection, which undoubtedly would lead to our involvement. They wanted us assigned to the case."

Phil: "It seems like an odd way to bring you out in the open. Why not just wait for the right opportunity to launch an attack? Using a political rally as a catalyst seems like an unnecessary step."

Ava: "Not if the smoke screen was intentional. We believe they wanted us looking in the wrong direction. With us distracted by a false political angle, it could give them the opening they needed. When they launched the rocket yesterday, we were following up a lead that was politically connected. They had their distraction and it nearly cost Gary Ceepo his life."

Roberta, showing a sigh of relief on her face: "I knew this could not be politically motivated. I told Phil that I could not imagine anyone, in either campaign, going that far."

Howie: "Does that mean we are no longer suspects?"

Ava: "Unless something surfaces to change our minds, neither your team nor Dan McGinnis's team remain on our radar. That does not mean that we don't need your help, however."

Phil: "What is it you need us to do?"

Ava: "We must keep the public and the media believing that the attacks are politically motivated. We cannot afford to let the terrorists suspect that we have moved on from that theory. We hope that they might let down their guard a little if they think we are still distracted, as we continue to search for them."

Liz: "Before you arrived, we were discussing the rocket attack that occurred yesterday. A member of your team, Gary Ceepo, was heading to Wayne to interview one of our volunteers. I suspect that the rocket attack had a lot to do with altering your opinion."

Ava: "You are correct, Liz. The rocket attack convinced us that we are the target. To get more specific, we believe the target is Jake Patrick."

Ava: "He was supposed to be in that car, not Gary Ceepo. We were the only people knowing Gary was taking Jake's place for the interview. Someone who knew where Jake was supposed to be yesterday had to inform the terrorists of his whereabouts at that particular moment. We are trying to figure that out."

Liz: "We obviously knew about the interview. Jake called us himself to inform us he planned on talking to our volunteer. Doesn't that suggest that our volunteer might be involved with the terrorists?"

Ava: "On the surface, that seems like a logical assumption but, as it turns out, he's the least likely suspect. Jake called to let him know that Gary would be conducting the interview. If he is tied to the terrorists, they would have known that Jake was not in that car."

Ava: "As for the interview itself, I'm afraid we were not as secretive as we should have been. Because of that, there were a number of ways they could have gotten information about Jake's schedule."

Phil: "What can we do to help you? Do you want us to do media interviews supporting the political angle?"

Ava: "That would help us immensely. We have a couple of leads to follow up that might get us closer to finding those responsible. Jake is not shy about exposing himself to danger if it helps us catch these people."

Ava: "Now that you are no longer suspects, we are in a better position to keep your team informed about our efforts to end this threat before anyone else gets hurt or killed."

Ava: "Here's where we stand at the moment and what we plan on doing to help end this nightmare."

Saturday, May 11th
Office of the NJ Special Projects Task Force
Morristown, NJ - 9:46AM

While Jake continues to study the street videos, a call comes in from Dennis McCollum, who is surveilling the religious store owner, Abdul Farouk: "I'm afraid we have a problem, Jake. Abdul Farouk is not here. The store remains closed, more than an hour after it was supposed to open."

Jake: "He lives upstairs, if our intel is correct. He may still be at home."

Dennis: "When the store remained closed, Mary Ellen and I became concerned. When I approached the store, there was a sign on the door that indicated that the store would re-open on Monday due to a family emergency. As far as we know, Abdul does not have any family in the states."

Dennis: "Out of options, we decided to take a risk by ringing his doorbell. There are four apartments in the building, so we had to be careful not to alert anyone else as to our intentions."

Dennis: "When no one responded to the doorbell, I let myself in, heading straight to his apartment. If he answered the door, I planned on pretending to be looking for his neighbor, accidentally knocking on the wrong door."

Dennis: "When no one acknowledged the knock, I broke into his apartment to find it empty. My instincts tell me he may have left for good. While the apartment was neat and orderly, the closet was fairly empty and all of the normal religious articles that devout muslims keep at home, such as his prayer rug, were missing. Who takes these items with them?"

Jake: "If he's left for good, we have a real problem. They may be closing ranks, with no plans to return to their lives in America."

Jake: "The traps we are setting were designed to bring them together so that we could eliminate the terror cell before any further damage is done. Without the ability to follow them, we lose the advantage."

————————————————————

The team's worst nightmare is now a reality. None of the three suspects can be located. Without a way of knowing where they are, they are free to plan without interference, leaving Jake and his team with a far dangerous mission.

The teams are going to have to protect both locations, not knowing which one might be at the center of a terror attack. They have gone from being the hunters to being the prey, with the only clue being the identity of a few of the terrorists, but not all.

They remain one step behind the terrorists, not a safe place to be.

Saturday, May 11th
Habib Residence
Fairfield, NJ - 10:24AM

_____

Josef Habib has just completed his phone call with the benefactor. He knows where Jake Patrick plans to be this afternoon at 3:00PM. They now have the opportunity to eliminate Jake Patrick, along with any of his team who find themselves close by.

Josef: "Today, we accomplish our mission, with plenty of time for us to make our flight to Germany. Our concern that the benefactor was going to fail us turned out to be unwarranted."

Abdul Farouk: "I think we ought to avoid celebrating too soon. Jake Patrick and his team have proven they are more than capable of protecting themselves. This plan of yours, Josef, better be a good one."

Mohammed Sarif: "I sense a lack of commitment on your part, Abdul. Are you not a loyal supporter of BAHRUN? We cannot place our own safety before the mission. To do so can make us less willing to do everything in our power to succeed. While we all want to stay alive, assuring that Jake Patrick does not, has to be our goal, no matter the outcome."

Alaina Assis: "Mohammed is correct. We have been given a gift by BAHRUN. They have chosen us to be the tip of the spear that needs to be placed in the heart of their most vile enemy. I can think of no greater honor than that, as a loyal jihadist?"

Josef Habib: "Let's not turn on each other. Abdul meant no harm. I'm sure all of us will do whatever is necessary to reach our goal. We have waited years for this opportunity to serve BAHRUN. We will all do our part to see this to the end."

Josef: "Now here is what we need to do."

Thirty Minutes Earlier

The benefactor is experiencing a roller coaster of emotions, finding themselves between a rock and a hard place. How did things go so far off course?

The call about to be made will place the life of Jake Patrick in great danger. In retrospect, it seems like a cowardly move, placing one's own life and safety ahead of another, especially someone that is not worthy of being targeted at all.

Jake Patrick is a hero, someone who has risked his own life trying to keep Americans safe. How did it come to this? How can I place my own safety above his? What type of coward does that?

As the benefactor continues to fight this internal battle, the end result is one of shame as the call is made.

Saturday, May 11th
Office of the NJ Special Projects Task Force
Morristown, NJ - 11:11AM

As everyone convenes at the office, they have some serious planning to do. With no one to follow, they have no choice but to protect both locations.

Jake: "We are going to have to split up in order to provide cover at both sites. We chose two outdoor venues in order to avoid putting more civilians at risk. Without a clue as to the whereabouts of our suspects, we are left with a different problem. How do we secure these locations without leaving our people unprotected?"

Jake: "Being out in the open was okay when we thought we could stop the attack before it began. I'm sorry that I ever asked for your help, Maddy."

Maddy: "Let's not waste time on apologies. We face danger every day."

Maddy: "Let's approach this from a position of strength rather than one of weakness. We have enough time to surveil the locations before Jake's arrival time. Being outdoors, we can be assured that our terrorists will not be able to plant explosives close enough to do any damage. That leaves the possibility of a sniper being the more likely method of attack."

Kent Baldauf: "Let's not forget the use of a rocket launcher. That can do significant damage and it doesn't require a direct hit in order to accomplish its objective."

Ava Matthews: "I wish we had more information before having to carry out this mission. We still do not know who is running the terror cell. Since we were not able to identify or place any of the three suspects in the area of the first attack, it goes without saying that the radical in charge might also be the sniper."

Dennis McCollum: "What you say is true but we are not without valuable intelligence. Both Kent and I, having extensive sniper training, are familiar with canvassing our surroundings before placing our teams in danger. I doubt these jihadists are skilled assassins. We could spot a threat a mile away. If the bad guys are nearby, we will find them."

Tricia: "We are using the male pronoun frequently. After having eliminated a female sniper recently, we cannot afford to be so sure that our missing sniper is male."

Jake: "You are talking about Linda Ventimiglia. Linda acted alone, not as part of an active terror cell. She may have used terrorists to her advantage but she was never a part of their jihad."

Jake: "I've never seen an Islamic terror cell run by a woman. With that said, I do agree we cannot take any chances. Anyone, male or female that appears to be suspicious, must be considered dangerous and a potential threat."

Jake: "I know its a big ask but does anyone wish to volunteer to pretend to be me?"

Tricia: "I'm willing but it may be hard to convince anyone I'm you. Our body types are slightly different."

As everyone smiles, Billy MacDonald decides to step up to the plate: "We are about the same height and built. I'm sure you can disguise me well enough to pull it off. I'm in if everyone is on board with it."

Maddy: "I'm sure we can make that work. On another front, we need to split Kent and Dennis up for the assignments as well. Our two snipers need to be canvassing the two locations for possible terror activity."

Jake: "We are down a man with Gary in the hospital but I think we can make this work. My wife, Keri Ann, insisted on helping us. She is a trained ex-marine, not without skills. I could not talk her out of participating, especially since I was going to be the target."

Jake: "Why don't we keep our teams in place? My team will handle the cemetery while Maddy's team can handle the park in Toms River."

Maddy: "Speaking of Gary, any news on his condition?"

Ava: "We got a call earlier from the doctors. The swelling in his brain remains problematic, requiring them to keep him sedated. They are still hopeful but he's far from out of the woods."

Maddy: "We all share your concerns. He's not without skills of his own, one of them is his heart. If Gary has a say in this, he will make a full recovery."

Mary Ellen Tremblay: "Before we get started, tell us how you decided on the two locations and what stories you fed to the political campaigns?"

Jake: "The park, where the first shot was fired, was an easy one. We pretended that the local authorities were able to discover a few irregularities at the park that might guide us in the right direction. I decided to go myself to examine the evidence that led to that phone call."

Jake: "As for the cemetery, one of our past team members, Michael Lemmo, is buried at Calvary Cemetery in Union, NJ. I visit his grave every year on the anniversary of his death. Today would be that day."

Maddy: "Both scenarios seem logical to me. I suggest we get to it."

As the teams prepare to leave, everyone knows the dangers that lie ahead. Without better intel they are going to have to rely on their skillsets and their instincts. They will just have to be better than the jihadists if they plan on returning home.

Chapter Fifteen

Stacking the Deck

Saturday, May 11th
An Unknown Location
Somewhere in New Jersey - 11:56AM

The benefactor is having an ongoing battle between conscience and ambition. Somehow, things have gone so far off course as to defy credibility. The plan to try and influence the outcome of a Senate race has turned into something entirely different.

How did I get myself into this mess? I guess fate has a way of insuring that we all pay for our mistakes, no matter the nature of the indiscretion.

I knew that what I was doing was wrong but I convinced myself that the end result was worth it. It's amazing how easy it is to fool oneself into believing that upsetting the apple cart would not result in harm to anyone.

Now that I have a decision to make, do I remain hidden, allowing this maniac to commit murder? Can I live with my choice, even if it ends in the death of a true American hero? How strong is my desire to protect my own interests?

Maybe there's a way to make things right without the risk of discovery? Is there a door that remains open that won't fly back at me?

The truth is, no matter what I do, it's hard to ignore the obvious. I'm a coward at heart.

Saturday, May 11th
Wayne General Hospital
Wayne, NJ - 12:09PM

The two doctors assigned to the care of Gary Ceepo are discussing his present condition. One is a neurosurgeon and the other is a well respected neurologist. All the other medical professionals involved in this case have completed their assignments, dealing with Gary's physical injuries as best they could. The remaining issue is still the most troublesome; the swelling of the brain.

Neurosurgeon: "The longer I wait to determine the damage, the less likely it is he will survive. We have to find a way to reduce the swelling. If I open the skull prematurely, we may win the battle but lose the war. The ancillary damage to him cannot be ignored."

Neurologist: "The safest way is for the swelling to begin to lessen on its own, indicating the body is beginning to heal itself."

Neurologist: "Using drugs to reduce the mass might allow you to get in but it could hide something far more dangerous. Before I can sign off on that, I want to give it a little more time. If we see no improvement by the morning, we will consider using the drugs. Let's hope it does not become necessary to do so."

Saturday, May 11th
McGinnis Campaign Headquarters
Middletown, NJ - 12:14PM

————————————————

Dan and Debbie McGinnis, along with their Chief of Staff, Robert O'Reilly, are gathered in Dan's office awaiting the latest polling data. They called this meeting for noon, knowing that the updated poll numbers were due to be released midday.

O'Reilly: "This moratorium on campaigning is going to hurt us the most. I'm convinced that when the numbers begin rolling in, we are going to see the gap narrow significantly. We need to find a way to talk to the voters directly."

Debbie: "I suspect that Phil Trooien might react differently, thinking this pause in the campaign might be hurting him more. If we begin closing the gap, the last thing the Senator will want to do is remain on the sidelines. He's been able to appear cavalier up until now. Having a ten point lead can be hard to overcome."

Dan: "The two of you are acting as if all of this is normal? This is far from normal. Better poll numbers will not do me any good if this madman succeeds in ending my life."

Dan, trying to calm his nerves before continuing: "I know that Jake Patrick and his team think these attacks were nothing but a smokescreen to get to him. Let's not forget that reflects his opinion, not fact. I'm not going to feel safe until this mess is over. I'm more than comfortable with avoiding public appearances for the time being."

As the three sit in silence, Laurie Duffy knocks on the door, calling out at the same time: "The polls are in and you are going to like the results."

As Laurie enters the office, her smile tells them everything they need to know. As she places the numbers in front of Dan, she can't help but comment: "The staff outside are jubilant. No one expected the numbers to be this good. The Senator has a real battle on his hands, one that we are more than willing to rage on your behalf."

As they study the results, the five major polls all show the same thing. The important one, Real Clear Politics, provides a better snapshot of the most realistic picture, as it is an average of all the polls conducted across the state.

O'Reilly: "Real Clear Politics shows us to be within 3 points of the Senator. That places us within the margin of error. We have picked up 7 points since the shooting. There's no longer any doubt that the sympathy vote is alive and well."

Debbie: "That's a big number Dan. I thought we would gain in the polls, but I did not expect this. How can we not comment to the media? There's got to be a way to acknowledge the change in the numbers without campaigning."

Dan: "We promised Jake Patrick that we would lay low while he searches for the person behind the attacks. Anything we say could shatter that trust."

Dan: "Do either of you think that speaking publicly would not force Phil Trooien to do likewise? The gloves would be off and the campaigns would have to continue as planned, as if nothing happened."

O'Reilly: "Now that we are gaining on him, would that be such a bad thing?"

Debbie: "I have to agree with Bob. No one says we have to place you in harm's way. We can stay away from any public appearances while communicating with the press from a safe distance. If Phil wants to get more aggressive, that will be up to him."

Dan: "I'm not happy about any of this but to ignore a request from the people trying to protect us, that's not something I'm comfortable doing."

O'Reilly: "I may have a back door way of getting the message across. Dakota Whalen from the Herald has been a key player in all of this. She digs deeper than any other reporter. I can ask her for help, requesting that she keep her source confidential."

Dan: "What exactly do you plan on telling her?"

O'Reilly: "I'll start with promising her an exclusive, once Jake Patrick removes the shackles. All she needs to do is pretend that she has had discussions with a number of voters who indicated that these attacks on Dan are having the opposite affect than the one intended. Instead of frightening voters away, they have pushed them closer to the Congressman."

O'Reilly: "After the latest poll results, the numbers will support her back story, so no harm, no foul."

Debbie: "In other words, you want her to lie in order to obtain the exclusive."

O'Reilly: "Lying is a little harsh, don't you think? Reporters exaggerate the truth all the time in order to enhance their stories. The new polls just confirm what we already know, Dan is gaining in support throughout the state."

Dan: "And you think that Dakota Whalen is the right reporter for you to contact about this?"

O'Reilly: "She's the most respected reporter in the state. Who better to get our message out to the public?"

Debbie: "Why not approach a lesser known journalist who is looking to make a name for themselves?"

O'Reilly: "And fail to have the message reach our intended target? If we are going to take the risk, let's make sure the message is heard."

Dan: "Okay, you can call her about this, but please be careful. If she seems reluctant, don't push it. We don't want her as an enemy. We are finally heading in the right direction, let's not put up any roadblocks."

Robert O'Reilly smiles to himself as he appears to have won this battle. He's already picturing himself being the Chief of Staff for the newest Senator on Capitol Hill, a position of power that he has coveted for a long time.

People tend to think that money is the ultimate goal for those looking to get ahead. While money is a nice bonus, it's the power that everyone seeks. Power is the ultimate aphrodisiac. It makes everything else pale in comparison.

O'Reilly: "I'll make the call this afternoon."

Saturday, May 11ᵗʰ
Trooien Residence
Bedminster, NJ - 12:21PM

———————————————

Phil Trooien is perusing the results from the latest polls, the first to be released since the initial attack on the Congressman. While he did expect to see McGinnis get a bump from the publicity, it's a lot worse than he expected.

While the Senator was in a strategy meeting with Howard Clarke and Liz Anderson, his wife, Roberta, was the first to see the polls on the news. She quickly pulled up the results on line and downloaded a copy.

It took her less than a minute to make her way, with the printout, into his office. While she may not be part of his re-election team, she remains Phil's biggest supporter. The results are telling her that he may need all the support he can get during these trying times.

Howard Clarke is the first to react to the polling news: "We all knew that the sympathy vote was a possibility. All this does is confirm it. Let's not forget that we are still in the lead. I think that says a lot about Phil's popularity with the New Jersey voters."

Phil, turning toward Howie: "There will be no spin in this room, this is a disaster. It took Dan four months of campaigning to pry away one point from me in the polls. Now, in less than two days, he's managed to pick up another seven, making this race a statistical tie. There is no spin that can camouflage the impact the attack has had on our campaign."

Roberta: "I cannot believe that the voters fail to see how superficial they are when they allow these attacks to alter their allegiance. Whoever this madman is, the person who has done the most for the citizens of New Jersey is Phil, not Dan McGinnis. I thought loyalty was a virtue worth preserving? This should not be happening."

Liz Anderson: "We have nearly six months to turn things around. That's a lifetime in politics. These issues will die down well before anyone has to vote. I'm convinced that we will have the support we need when the time comes."

Howie: "To be honest, having to pause our campaign has left us without a means of communicating with the voters. McGinnis gets the bump and we have to remain silent. There has to be a way of getting our message out without violating our agreement?"

Roberta: "Now that we know that neither political party is behind the attacks, it makes sense to cancel the pause and let everyone get back to campaigning. The voters need to hear from everyone before they get entrenched with one candidate, especially because of a mis-directed attack."

Phil: "The information that Jake's team shared with us is not to leave this office. They told us that in confidence. The key to letting him do his job is to keep the public believing that the attacks are politically motivated. While he may not be my favorite person right now, I'm not going to go against his wishes."

Phil: "Finding the terrorists responsible is more important than trying to sway public opinion in our favor. There will be plenty of time to right the ship once the threat is over."

The Senator, along with his team, settle in to plan how they intend on continuing their campaign once the restraints are lifted. Hopefully, the NJ Special Projects Task Force can capture those responsible before anyone else gets hurt.

As for the Senate race, once the voters find out that the attacks were not politically motivated, there's a better than average chance things will get back to normal. Hopefully, that time is not too far away.

Saturday, May 11th
Offices of the New Jersey Herald
Hackensack, NJ - 1:06PM

Dakota Whalen has had an unexpected setback. Her planned meeting over drinks with Laurie Duffy was canceled at the last minute when the car bomb exploded near Middletown, NJ. Laurie called it off as everyone in her office turned their attention to the well being of the Congressman.

After the bombing, Dakota decided to change direction by arranging for a number of personal interviews with locals near the attack sites. She even managed to get an appointment with the gentleman that was tackled at the rally. He got more than he bargained for when he tried to get his wife a photo of the congressman.

While putting together her newly revamped schedule, her desk phone rings, something it rarely does. Most calls from her office are self generated. The main switchboard rarely lets calls come through without prior clearance.

Dakota, picking up the phone: "This is Dakota Whalen. How can I help you?"

Robert O'Reilly: "Ms. Whalen, It's nice to finally talk to you."

Dakota: "It's Mrs. Whalen. And you are?"

O'Reilly: "Oh, I'm sorry, I should have started with that piece of information. I'm Robert O'Reilly, Chief of Staff for Congressman Daniel McGinnis."

Dakota: "Are you sure you reached the right person? I'm not the political journalist for the Herald, I'm an investigative reporter. I can try and transfer you but please understand that I'm not an expert on our phone system so you may wind up in the wrong place."

O'Reilly: "There's been no mistake Dakota. Can I call you Dakota?"

Dakota: "That's my name."

O'Reilly: "I wanted to compliment you on the article you wrote after the shooting. Your insight into the shooter was quite extraordinary. While the other journalists were chasing their tails, you were able to get to the heart of the matter. How did you manage to find the point of attack?"

Dakota: "Mr. O'Reilly, while I appreciate the compliment, this conversation is a bit perplexing. I understand that both campaigns for the Senate seat are temporarily shut down while Jake Patrick conducts his investigation. What is the real reason for this call?"

O'Reilly: "Now I know why you are such a successful journalist. Your'e obviously not a fan of the conversational dance."

Dakota: "I'm not a very good dancer. As for how I approach my job, the less time spent on nonsense, the better. What is it you want from me?"

O'Reilly: "Can I assume that your interest in these attacks on Congressman McGinnis remain an ongoing story for you?"

Dakota: "While I have little interest in the world of politics, I can't help believe that these attacks transcend Dan McGinnis's job. While others may treat these attacks superficially, I tend to dig a lot deeper. My instincts tell me that the bad guys behind these attacks have more on their agenda than politics. I refuse to accept things only on face value."

O'Reilly: "Now we can get to the reason for my call. Without revealing anything that we have sworn to keep private, Jake Patrick and his team have uncovered information that suggests there is more to this than meets the eye. Your instincts are correct."

O'Reilly: "While you may not care about the politics, it's all I can think about. After the attacks, the worst course of action for us is silence. We need to get to the voters

without violating our agreement to remain in the background. The public needs to know how committed Dan is to becoming their Senator. They must know that these attacks have not softened his resolve. In fact, they have strengthened it."

Dakota: "What does that have to do with me?"

O'Reilly: "You are one of the more respected journalist in the state. In return for you helping us, we are willing to offer you an exclusive interview, one that will blow the doors off of everything that goes on behind the curtain during a campaign, including confidential information about the attacks."

Dakota: "And when will this exclusive interview take place?"

O'Reilly: "According to Jake Patrick, it's only a matter of days before things can get back to normal. As soon as that happens, we will talk to no one until we meet with you."

Dakota: "Okay, let's assume I'm interested. What can I do that might get your message across without jeopardizing your promise to remain silent?"

O'Reilly: "We would like you to publish an article about the attacks, something you are, most likely, already planning to do. In that article, we would like you to include reference to a number of New Jersey citizens who have rallied behind Dan after the attempts on his life."

O'Reilly: "You can mention how they have been angered by the attacks and how brave Dan has been, a trait they find to be patriotic. Based on the recent polls, his support has been growing, which makes your comments match perfectly with the latest numbers."

After a few moments of silence, Dakota responds: "So you want me to lie?"

O'Reilly: "What we are asking you to do is remind the public that there is a campaign going on. Obviously, Dan's gaining support based on the polls. There's little doubt that this upswing in his numbers originated from the attacks. All we are asking you to do is remind the voters of that fact. It's a small price to pay for an exclusive."

Dakota: "I must say you have given me a lot to think about. Let me digest this in greater detail. I will let you know by tomorrow."

O'Reilly: "As long as you do not discuss this with anyone, we can wait until tomorrow."

As Dakota hangs up the phone, her mind is going at lightning speed. What just happened?

She knows politics is a brutal game. With a number of people killed and dozens more injured, it appears that our politicians are a lot more egotistical than she realized. When in pursuit of power, everything else, including injury and death, is nothing more than collateral damage.

For the first time since the shooting, Dakota is considering the unthinkable. Could these politicians be behind the attacks? After what she just heard, It's a distinct possibility.

Chapter Sixteen

Its Time to Take Control

Saturday, May 11th
Office of the NJ Special Projects Task Force
Morristown, NJ - 1:13PM

As the two teams prepare to leave the office, Tricia Highland returns with sandwiches from the local deli. Everyone is going to have to eat on the run but ignoring one's hunger would be a mistake.

Tricia: "Before we go, I thought this was worth mentioning. There's a young man sitting across the street in his car. He appears to be waiting for someone."

Jake: "I suspect that there is more to it if you are bringing it up. What peaked your interest?"

Tricia: "I'm sure I saw him earlier this morning, sitting where he is right now."

Kent: "Maybe I should go out and ask him? What does he look like?"

Tricia: "He appears to be of middle eastern descent, not much older than his late teens or early twenties. I have to admit that it was his apparent heritage that caught my eye this morning. Not wanting to come across as being paranoid, I forgot all about it until now."

Billy: "For him to be sitting outside for hours, I doubt this is a coincidence. If I had to guess, he could be part of the terror cell we are trying to shut down. If they are after Jake, as we suspect they are, keeping tabs of his movements would make logical sense."

Jake: "If Billy's right, we may be able to use this to our advantage."

Kent: "The best way for us to learn his intentions would be to have everyone leave the office except Jake. If he follows Jake when he leaves, we have our answer."

Mark: "If he fails to follow any of us, we can double back and get behind him without being seen."

Kent: "In other words, the prey becomes the hunter."

Jake: "Let's do it. We can't leave for our assignments until we know for sure. Tricia, where is he parked?"

Tricia: "He's sitting in front of the Dry Cleaners in a white Toyota sedan. The car looks to be about 10 years old. We have to make sure that we don't spook him or we may lose him for good."

Kent: "If it turns out that he's one of the bad guys, how do you want to handle this?"

Jake: "We let him follow me for a mile or two. I suspect he will contact his superior that he is on the move. That has to be the last call he makes before we grab him. We have to be quick and thorough."

Ava: "There's a park a few miles away that we have to drive past on our way to the Parkway. With no residences or businesses on that street, the parking spaces are usually empty. Jake can pull over, causing him to do so as well. That will give us a short window to take him down."

Jake: "I'd like Kent to take him back to the office for interrogation. It could help us immensely if he can get him to talk. The more intel we have the better before we have to interact with his fellow jihadists."

Kent: "I can do that, no problem. Whatever he knows, we will know. This is not my first rodeo."

Jake: "Remember Kent, this is not Afghanistan. You need to make sure that the threat is sufficient to get him to talk."

Kent: "It's all in how you get your point across. If he believes that I will not hesitate to act, that should be enough."

Jake: "I will have our local police chief arrange to have a couple of his detectives meet you at the office after you had some time to converse with him. They can baby sit him while we allow our plan play out."

Maddy's team is the first to leave the office. Her car is parked near the corner, about 50 feet from the suspect's car. As the team of Madeline Hampton, Mark Moorhead, Dennis McCollum, Billy MacDonald and Mary Ellen Tremblay leave the building, everyone takes a quick glance at the suspect.

As they pull away from the curb, there is no movement on the part of the man in the white Toyota. So far, things are preceding as expected.

The next to leave are Kent Baldauf, Ava Matthews and Tricia Highland. Jake's wife, Keri Ann, is meeting everyone near the cemetery.

After identifying the suspects whereabouts, they get into the car, slowly leaving the curb. Ava has Maddy's phone on speaker as they drive away. Maddy's team has already circumnavigated the block and is observing the white Toyota: "He's made no attempt to move his car. He's waiting for Jake."

Ava: "It looks like we have a terrorist to capture."

Jake answers on the first ring: "Jake, you were right. The kid is still parked outside. He's waiting for you. How do you want to play this?"

Jake: "I'll leave the office and head west toward the Garden State Parkway. We will do the take down as we discussed. Let's hope the parking spaces are empty."

Kent, over the speaker: "Our plan is workable. He has no idea what is about to hit him."

Prior to leaving, Jake calls his wife, Keri Ann, to let her know what is happening: "It appears we have one of the terrorist following me. We should have him under control shortly. With any luck, he will turn out to be talkative, making our assignment less problematical."

Keri Ann Patrick: "How often do you get that lucky? At least there will be one less terrorist to deal with at the cemetery."

Jake: "We're not even sure the cemetery will be the target. Billy MacDonald is going to pretend to be me in Toms River Centennial Park. Based on what we know, it's still a 50/50 chance either way."

Keri Ann: "We have two good teams handling both sites. Whatever team faces the terrorists, the bad guys will be at a disadvantage."

Jake: "This is a distraction that we do not need right now."

Keri Ann: "I disagree. Capturing one of the terrorists, who may provide some valuable intelligence, is far superior than no intelligence."

Jake: "Of course you're right. I'm about to leave the office. I'll call you either way." As Jake ends the call, he heads for the front door, hoping to end this minor distraction on a positive note.

Saturday, May 11th
Sitting in the White Toyota
Morristown, NJ - 1:23PM

————————————————————

While watching the teams leave the office, the young *Terrorist in Training* decides to call Josef Habib with an update: "I'm looking at the second car of agents leaving the office. So far, Jake Patrick must still be inside. What do you want me to do?"

Habib: "You must keep your attention on Jake Patrick. According to my source, he will be leaving soon. You have to follow him no matter where he's headed. If he's not coming toward me, as we were told, we will need time to react."

Habib, realizing that he is putting a great deal of responsibility on a young neophyte: "Your commitment to our cause tells me that you will make a fine jihadist, my friend. As we have discussed, your willingness to risk your life for the greater good of the jihad, is a key part of your enlightenment."

Habib: "As for your present assignment, the threat of death should not be on the table. Today, you will take your first steps toward immortality by being our eyes and ears. All that matters is not losing sight of Jake Patrick, do you understand?"

Young Jihadist: "I will do my part, you have my word."

After ending the call, he starts the engine for the first time in hours. He knows that nothing can distract him once Jake Patrick makes his appearance. All that matters is showing Habib that his faith in him is justified.

Saturday, May 11th
McGinnis Campaign Headquarters
Middletown, NJ - 1:24PM

————————————————

Robert O'Reilly's anxiety level is increasing rapidly. The more he replays his conversation with Dakota Whalen in his head, the more concerned he is that the call was a mistake. He has yet to return to Dan's office, hoping to get his emotions in check before having to discuss the call.

Bob knows that the first question Dan will ask will be about the phone call. He needs to gather his thoughts and find a way to hide his concerns before exposing himself to his colleagues.

Why is he experiencing such doubt? There was nothing said to indicate that Dakota was dismissing his proposal outright. I guess it all comes down to tone. He had to admit that she was less than enthusiastic about his offer, even the possibility of an exclusive interview.

Unfortunately, what's done is done. He has no choice but to spin it in a positive light.

As O'Reilly returns to Dan's office, the Congressman and his wife are digging deeper into the polling results, trying to better understand the reason behind their bump in the polls.

When digesting poll results, how you present the questions can have a lot to do with the answers you receive. Asking the same question two different ways can skew the polls as much as 10%, depending on the bias of the question.

As Bob takes a seat, Debbie is the first to respond: "We have been studying the polls and, if we are correct, this is looking better than I might have suspected. If you take the Quinnipiac poll, they presented the question simply and without bias."

Who do you prefer in the upcoming Senatorial Election?

"That poll saw a jump in support of Dan from 43% to the present number of 47%, while Phil declined from 53% to 51%, leaving him with just a 4 point lead. You can't ask that question more fairly than they did and we still knocked it out of the park."

Dan: "The more I study it the better it looks. We may have been too hasty looking for a way to get our message out to the voters. With both campaigns on the sidelines, we are benefiting the most."

Debbie, turning toward O'Reilly: "Speaking of reaching out to the voters, were you able to talk to Dakota Whalen?"

Bob: "I reached her at her office and the conversation went well. She seemed quite excited about getting an exclusive interview with Dan. She asked for a day to think it over but I'm confident that we were of the same mind about this."

Dan: "I don't want you to call her again. Let her reach out to you. Before I agree to this, I want to be sure that she is totally on board. She has to make the next move or we let the whole thing lie."

Bob: "I understand. If she does call me, how do you want me to proceed?"

Dan: "I'll talk to her before we go any further. If I sense any reluctance or hesitation, I will shut it down completely. In return for her keeping our talk confidential, I will agree to the exclusive interview when the pause has been lifted without her having to do anything at all. I can't see her objecting to that?"

Bob: "Let's see what happens."

As all three continue their discussion, Bob's anxiety is still heading north.

It's taking all of his resolve to keep it hidden from the team. He knows that Dakota's failure to respond is a lot more problematic than Dan might suspect. Having an experienced journalist suspecting Dan of trying to gain an edge by compromising the journalist's integrity, is not the end of the story, just the beginning.

Saturday, May 11th
Jake Patrick's Car
Heading Toward Union NJ - 1:43PM

As he leaves the office, Jake's pretending to be on his phone, oblivious to his surroundings. The last thing he wants to do is catch his prey off guard.

After starting the car, he pulls away from the curb, catching the white Toyota in the rear view mirror. Before he can get more than a few feet, he sees the Toyota pulling away from the curb as well.

All doubt has been lifted. They have settled on a plan and now it needs to be carried out to optimal precision. They will only get one chance to capture him before he can send a distress signal.

A few miles away from the park, Jake calls Ava Matthews, who is handling all communications: "Ava, do you have a clear view of our jihadist?"

Ava: "He's right in front of us. Maddy's car is leaving the caravan in order to get herself into position."

Jake: "Good, Let's hope there's plenty of room for us to pull over."

Ava: "The plans a good one, we will subdue him quickly."

As Jake sees the park off to his left, he begins slowing down, pretending that there's something wrong with his car. He can see the white Toyota in his rear view mirror, trying to stay two cars behind him.

As he pulls over toward the curb, he pops the hood for all to see. He can see the Toyota slow down as well, moving toward the curb with two cars parked between his car and Jake's, providing him with a little cover.

As Jake exits the car to further open the hood, Dennis McCollum is advancing, out of view, toward the driver's side of the Toyota. Meanwhile, Mary Ellen is approaching the passenger side of the car.

Without warning, she knocks on the glass as the jihadist, startled by the intrusion, looks in her direction. Before he can react, Dennis smashes the driver's side window, as he reaches in, grabbing him before he can make a move.

As Dennis drags him through the broken window, he holds him on the ground, preventing any movement, while covering his mouth to avoid any further disturbance.

The entire altercation takes less than 25 seconds. The terrorist's phone remains in the car on the passenger seat, silent and no longer a threat.

Mission accomplished.

Jake: "We need to act fast, before the police arrive. Kent, you take my car back to the office with our friend secured in the back. I'll wait to call the local police until I reach the cemetery. That should give you a good half hour to get some intel out of him."

Kent: "That long? I might learn the names of every member of his family in that time."

Jake: "Remember, threats, not physical contact. We don't need any trouble with law enforcement."

Kent: "Just leave it to me."

As Kent, Dennis and Mark secure their prey before placing him in the car, Tricia cleans out the white Toyota, removing everything that might be of informational value. She then gets back in her car, along with Jake and Ava, as all three vehicles leave the area.

While there are a number of citizens looking on from a distance, not quite sure of what they are seeing, the team is long gone, less than 5 minutes after they arrived.

There will be plenty of time, after things settle down, for Jake to fill in the blanks for the authorities. As for now, they need to prepare for the potential assault that might be coming their way. Maybe our young jihadist can fill in some of the missing pieces.

Chapter Seventeen

———————————————————

Preparing to Wake the Dead

Saturday, May 11ᵗʰ
The New Jersey Herald
Hackensack, NJ - 1:51PM

———————————————————

It appears that Dakota's approach to the attacks have taken a complete one-eighty. Everything changed after receiving that phone call.

Her conversation with Congressman Daniel McGinnis's Chief of Staff, Robert O'Reilly, has her considering a different angle, as she contemplates the number one story in the state right now. Every newspaper, broadcast media and on line internet site are obsessed with the recent attacks aimed at Congressman Daniel McGinnis.

Dakota planned to interview eyewitnesses to the attacks and getting their reactions. She now has set her sights on looking into the motives behind the attacks themselves, which might not be as obvious as everyone suspects.

Her instincts have always been the key to how she approaches any story. There's the obvious, something everyone can see and hear with their own eyes and ears, and the not so obvious, what might lie just beneath the surface.

Dakota's instincts are now telling her that there's more to see here. Obviously, Robert O'Reilly does not know her very well, if he thought he could tempt her into abandoning her ethics in return for an interview. By doing so, he opened a door she never knew existed.

The last person she would have suspected of trying to disobey Jake Patrick's orders was the Congressman that was the target of the attacks.

Just a few days removed from unspeakable tragedy, Dakota would think that Dan McGinnis would be hiding away, silent to a fault, concerned more with his own safety. She did not expect him to be actively pursuing his campaign for Senator while the attacker is still at large.

Over the years, politicians have gone to extremes to remain in power or obtain power.

There are no shortage of stories regarding failed attempts when reaching for the brass ring. The political graveyard is filled with people who decided to push the envelope of legality and decency, only to end up in obscurity.

Could it be possible that these attacks on Congressman McGinnis were staged in order for him to bridge the gap between his numbers and those of Senator Trooien? While the voters may not be beacons of knowledge when it comes to the issues, they can emotionally react when the situation calls for it.

Every politician, and every journalist, knows that the sympathy card is real and powerful. That's why we hear politicians constantly bringing up anyone in their family that has been hit with a hardship, no matter how much of a stretch it may be.

Did their parents suffer through the Depression? Was their childhood less than stellar? Did they lose a child or sibling to a tragedy? Every angle that might raise the emotional scale in their favor is free game in the arena of politics.

For the time being, Dakota Whalen has altered her course by turning her attention to finding the underlying connection between the attackers and the candidate. She now believes they are linked in some way.

As for getting back to Robert O'Reilly, she will wait as long as possible before telling him exactly what he can do with his offer. As soon as she can make sense of this unexpected turn of events, a call to Jake Patrick will be at the top of her list.

Jake has proven to be a professional that accepts nothing on face value. She would be surprised to learn that he's unaware that politics is indeed, alive and well. If she can fill in some of the blanks for him, he may be able to complete the puzzle.

For now, Dakota needs to discover the real reason O'Reilly made that call. Could it be that he was less concerned with McGinnis's safety because he knew he was never in any real danger?

Saturday, May 11th
Calvary Cemetery
Union, NJ - 1:58PM

––––––––––––––––––––––––

It's hard to find a more perfect day than today. The sun is shining, the temperature is mild and the humidity is non-existent. In fact, this might be the best day so far this spring.

While the cemetery can get crowded on the weekend, it appears that no one wants to do anything that takes them away from such a perfect day. There are few people making the trek to visit their departed love ones, a blessing in disguise based on what is about to occur.

Josef Habib and his fellow jihadists are preparing for the assault that is to come. As soon as they confirmed where Jake Patrick was heading, they made their way here to prepare for his arrival.

In addition to his three fellow jihadists, Habib has recruited two additional low level loyalists who are willing to put their lives on the line in order to serve BAHRUN.

Josef is well aware that the plan he has put together to rid the world of Jake Patrick will, mostly likely, lead to the death of his loyal but naive supporters. They will be rewarded in the afterlife for their loyalty and courage. Their sacrifice is a small price to pay for Habib succeeding in his mission.

Anyone that might be recognized on sight will remain hidden until the attack begins. He feels confident that Abdul Farouk, as well as the two new loyalists, will not be faces Jake Patrick knows, so they will be placed accordingly.

His two new loyalists are now wearing the uniforms of the maintenance staff while Abdul Farouk will be waiting for Jake's arrival at the entrance, as he takes the place of the security guard at the gate.

Habib knows that Mohammed Sarif has had his picture plastered all over the news, being the driver of the SAME DAY DELIVERY truck that saved the Congressman from injury at the site of the blast.

Anyone studying the surveillance cameras in Wayne, NJ, where the rocket was launched, might know that Mohammed is more than just a concerned citizen. It's quite possible that they caught a view of a SAME DAY DELIVERY van leaving the area.

It's also conceivable that the surrounding traffic cameras could have picked up Alaina Assis, who was the lookout that day. That leaves Abdul to be the one to come face to face with their target when he makes his way inside the gate.

When Habib arrived at the cemetery, there were just a few workers on duty that needed to be dealt with before they could put their plan in motion. As for those working in the main office, on the other side of the cemetery, they owe their lives to being far away from the action.

The first order of business for Habib was to go to the office and get directions to Michael Lemmo's gravesite. When he discovered that there were only three people

inside, he thought it best to leave the office staff alone. The last thing he needed was to have visitors enter the office and find no one to help them.

After locating the gravesite and studying the surroundings, he put the rest of his plan in motion.

He could see flags surrounding a vacant plot of land, not far from the grave of Michael Lemmo. A new gravesite will soon be prepped for the cemetery's newest arrival.

After gathering shovels from the maintenance shed, BAHRUN'S new loyalists will pretend to be working on the new gravesite. They will have two automatic rifles hidden under their equipment.

Because it is heavily wooded between themselves and their target, it will be a miracle if they succeed in taking down Jake Patrick. All they need to do is force him to retreat farther away from them, sending him closer to Habib and his imminent death.

Josef Habib has placed the cemetery's maintenance truck near a row of mausoleums at the far end of the cemetery, about 200 yards from the gravesite. It's far enough away to be clear of anyone that might be canvassing the area but well within range of the rocket launcher that will do his bidding.

When the firing starts, and Jake Patrick is forced to head away from the onslaught, he will be closing the gap between the bullets heading his way and his ultimate fate. Until the time to act arrives, Habib will hide in the rear of the maintenance truck.

The most important part of the plan is to avert everyone's attention away from the truck. Once Jake Patrick comes within 100 yards, he will begin receiving fire from a number of positions, forcing him to direct his attention elsewhere.

Mohammed Sarif will be stationed at the far end of the mausoleums, about 30 yards from the truck. Alaina Assis will begin firing from her post on top of the maintenance building, approximately 100 yards to the south of his position.

As for Abdul Farouk, he will leave his post at the entrance gate once Jake Patrick has entered the cemetery. He will begin firing from behind the highest tombstone in the area, the one with a six foot statue of Michael the Archangel, guarding the grave of another less known Michael.

The plan is to have Jake Patrick stop in his tracks, forcing him to engage his attackers. While he is distracted, Habib will exit the truck and end his life in a large ball of fire. An enemy of this magnitude cannot leave this world in a whimper.

Habib expects there to be others accompanying Jake to the gravesite. Trapping as many of them as possible in the rocket's kill zone will be a bonus that BAHRUN will celebrate for years to come.

Josef Habib is a realist. Jake Patrick and his team are a formidable bunch. Every member of his attack team might not make it past the first few minutes of the assault. All he needs for them to do is stay alive long enough for him to make his appearance while Jake and his team's attention is focused elsewhere.

As for Josef himself, while he may have the best chance to make it out alive, his odds are not that good. If every member of Jake's support team happens to make it into the kill zone, his odds increase significantly but that is far from a guarantee.

Josef Habib knows that his life may end today. As long as he succeeds in his mission, his rewards in the next life will be many. Today, he places his fate in the hands of Allah as he waits to complete his mission.

Saturday, May 11th
Office of the NJ Special Projects Task Force
Morristown, NJ - 2:02PM

As Kent Baldauf escorts his prisoner into the rear conference room, he places him in a chair, his hands tied behind his back. To avoid any possibility of him trying a counter move, he secures his hands and feet to the chair with zip ties. Let's see him try to escape carrying a heavy conference room chair that might weigh more than he does.

The young terrorist remained silent during the entire trip from the park. That was fine with Kent, who had no desire to interact until he was ready to do so. Now that he has him secured, his prisoner decides that he might as well begin the discussion phase: "I want a lawyer."

Kent ignores him for the time being as he goes around the conference room, closing all of the blinds that provide visual contact with the outside world.

Terrorist: "I said a want a lawyer. I have rights. You can't ignore me."

Kent ignores him, once again, as he prepares the conference room.

The first thing Kent does is place a large plastic drop cloth around the prisoner's chair, large enough to extend a good five feet in all directions. As he's doing so the prisoner reacts: "What the hell is this? Do you expect me to wet my pants? You don't scare me, this is a waste of time. Besides, I'm not saying anything until my lawyer arrives."

Kent continues to ignore him as he reaches into the duffle bag that he carried from the car. He removes a cloth bag and places it on the table. As he pulls back the cloth, the bag contains a number of knives, picks and hammers, all old, worn and obviously seen a lot of use over the years.

Terrorist: "Is that supposed to scare me? You can't touch me. I'll sue your ass off. Once my lawyer gets here, all this garbage will end. I demand you call the public defender's office and get me that lawyer!"

As Kent continues to ignore him, he places a few more objects on the conference table, including syringes and a few different glass tubes of liquids. The final object placed on the table is a uniquely designed pair of pliers with a sharp pointed edge rather than the typical snub nose design.

As he completes his preparation, Kent takes a seat across from the terrorist and calmly begins explaining how this interrogation will play out: "For some reason you must think that I'm a member of law enforcement. Let me assure you that I'm not."

Kent: "As for that lawyer you keep asking for, no one will be coming. The team that abducted you are part of a black ops unit that handles terror related cases. We have our own set of rules and they do not include lawyers, personal rights or any of that nonsense. All of that changed after 9/11. When it comes to terrorism, nothing is off the table."

The terrorist, looking less confident than before: "There's no way the United States Government would allow you to do any of this. We have certain rights that you can't ignore."

Kent, smiling from ear to ear: "You mean the rights that none of your extreme radical jihadists ever extend to **YOUR** victims? Oh, that's right, you count on these rights being one sided. To paraphrase an old saying *rights for me, but not for thee.*"

Kent: "How do you think we have succeeded these past years in shutting down so many terror assaults and planned attacks? Do you think we accomplished that by allowing the rules of a free nation to dictate our actions?"

Kent: "After 9/11, the government got smart and realized that the only way to win the war on terror was to play by their rules, not ours. Too many people would die if we allowed your fellow jihadists to be granted the same rights that our citizens enjoy."

The young radical is now showing signs of extreme concern: "This can't be happening. The public outcry would never permit you to do this?"

Kent: "That's why our unit is classified as black ops. Have you ever seen one of those James Bond movies? He was a British agent that had what they called a **LICENSE TO KILL**. While the movies may have been fiction, such a classification exists and we happen to have a free pass to do whatever is necessary in order to stop a terrorist attack."

Kent: "My time overseas in Afghanistan and Iraq had me responsible for obtaining information from known radical jihadists who threatened American lives. The tools of my trade, which are on the table, worked to perfection more often than not."

Kent: "I must say that, on occasion, a few of your fellow jihadists managed to avoid talking under duress. While that did not prevent me from continuing my efforts, none of those who failed to talk survived the attempt."

Kent: "Being a patriotic American, I never tortured anyone before explaining what was about to happen if they didn't talk. The lucky ones chose conversation while the unlucky ones paid a heavy price for their silence."

Kent: "The sad part is none of them lasted very long. They could have saved themselves a great deal of pain and damage if they agreed before hand. I never hurt anyone before giving them a chance to do the right thing. Unfortunately for many of them, actions spoke louder than words."

The young terrorist is now in full panic mode. He's beginning to move around as if such gyrations were going to keep Kent from proceeding. The horror on his face tells a different story than it did a few moments ago.

Kent: "Okay, let's begin. Here's the one and only time I'm going to use words rather than actions. I promised you a warning and I always keep my word. After that, there will be no more talking until you decide you had enough. For your sake, I hope you do not wait too long to come to that decision."

Saturday, May 11th
Approx. 10-12 minutes from Calvary Cemetery
Union, NJ - 2:28PM

The team will be meeting up with Jake's wife, Keri Ann, at the Union Diner, a five minute ride from the cemetery. It is there where they will decide on a course of action once they enter Calvary.

As Jake finds himself minutes from the diner, his phone rings. He can see that the call is coming from Kent Baldauf.

Jake: "I hope your interrogation was successful. It looks like you didn't need the whole half hour?"

Kent: "Actually, it was more like 18 minutes. He folded like a cheap suit in no time."

Jake: "I'm sorry but I did not have time to make the call to the local police."

Kent: "It's all taken care of. I'm already on my way to the cemetery. He's being held in the conference room while a couple of officers are guarding him. Unfortunately, he knew very little, which was not surprising."

Jake: "Is there anything that might help us?"

Kent: "The leader of the terror cell is a man named Josef Habib. He's a retired businessman living in Fairfield, New Jersey."

Kent: "He's the only person our friend had contact with and he's the one who radicalized him. As for where he is at the moment, the kid had no idea. His job was to follow you and relay your whereabouts."

Kent: "What the kid knew or didn't know is of no importance right now. By hacking his phone, we obtained Josef Habib's burner phone number, which places him somewhere in Union New Jersey. It looks like the assignment of capturing these guys will be on us."

Jake: "That also tells us which political team is responsible for this mess but we will deal with that later. Before heading to the cemetery, meet us at the Union Diner. Our strategy session has just gotten a lot more serious."

Kent: "I called Bill Greger at the FBI. He's looking into this Habib fellow as we speak. Maybe he can find out something that might give us an edge."

Jake: "Call him back and see if he can provide you with a photo of the guy. While we have little time to wait for information, knowing what our radical leader looks like could help save our lives."

Kent: "I'll take care of it. I'll be there shortly, so wait until I arrive before getting into the juicy details of how we are going to end this."

Chapter Eighteen

Whistling Past the Graveyard

Saturday, May 11ᵗʰ
The Union Diner
Union, NJ - 2:43PM

As the team arrives at the diner, Keri Ann Patrick is already seated in a booth in the back. She chose a large one in the rear of the diner that can handle six to seven patrons.

With this being an off time, the diner is fairly empty. While there are a few people eating, they are congregated around the counter or in one of the front booths facing the parking lot. They are free to converse without having to worry about being overheard.

As they all sit, the waitress arrives immediately to handle their needs. Jake decides to limit activity by flashing her his official credentials: "If we can all have coffee, that will suffice. We would appreciate it if you could allow us some privacy."

The waitress's facial expression indicates that she understands his request: "I'll get the coffee and then I'll make sure that you are left alone. If you need anything, please let me know."

Jake speaks first: "On the plus side, Kent had no problem getting the young radical to talk. As we all know, Kent can be very persuasive. On the negative side, he knows very little. Being a low level foot soldier, I'm sure his intel would not extend beyond the scope of his responsibility."

Tricia: "He must know something?"

Jake: "It appears that the leader of the terror cell is a jihadist by the name of Josef Habib. A quick search indicated that he is a retired businessman that presently lives in

Fairfield, NJ. Federal agents are heading there as we speak but I suspect they will not find him at home."

Ava: "Do we know what he looks like?"

Jake: "Bill Greger at the FBI will be getting us his photo shortly. That's about the only piece of intel that will do us any good right now."

Keri Ann: "What was his assignment?"

Jake: "He was told to follow me, not to engage. I suspect that his last phone call to Habib reinforced the fact that I was heading in this direction. They will be expecting us."

Ava: "Should we contact Maddy and let her know that we appear to be the target?"

Jake: "Since she is too far away to do us any good, let her remain and carry out her plan just in case we received false intel."

Keri Ann: "That's the smart play. To take the word of a terrorist at face value would be a mistake. With that said, we have to go with what we know. It appears that the terror cell plans on taking us out at the cemetery. How do we counter the attack?"

As they are about to get into the details, Kent Baldauf arrives at the diner, taking a seat next to Tricia: "What did I miss?"

Jake: "We are just getting started. If we are to assume that our prisoner was telling you the truth, we can expect to be attacked at the cemetery."

Kent: "Believe me, he was not lying. If he knew the medical history of Josef Habib, he would have spilled the beans entirely. I convinced him he was minutes away from serious harm. His loyalty to BAHRUN was secondary to his own personal well being."

Jake: "Then we have a job to do. We must pretend we are ignorant of the threat, while we conduct our own counter offensive. I have a few ideas but we need everyone's input before we head to Calvary Cemetery."

As the team settles in to formulate a plan, they are aware that time is not on their side. Habib might already suspect something, assuming he tried to contact his young loyalist and came up empty. If Habib suspects Jake's team is aware of their presence, he will adjust accordingly.

Nothing can be more dangerous than facing an enemy that knows you are heading their way.

Saturday, May 11ᵗʰ
Undisclosed Location
Somewhere in NJ - 2:48PM

————————————————

The Benefactor is heading for a total emotional breakdown.

Jake Patrick is just minutes away from facing a terrible onslaught that has him personally in the crosshairs of a terror attack bent on ending his life.

The benefactor is waging a personal battle between exposure and the desire to do the right thing.

Should I make the call to warn him? Once I expose myself, there will be no turning back. Would a call this late in the game be of any help? Could I live with myself if a true American hero ends up dead?

It's obvious that the benefactor is conflicted. The possibility of going to prison is bad enough, but it pales in comparison to the personal destruction that will certainly follow.

I can't help thinking that there is a third option. I have always wondered how someone could end their own life? What could possibly be so bad as to allow such thoughts to dictate one's actions?

Does it make me weak to be considering taking a coward's way out? The conflicting thoughts that are consuming my consciousness has me, for the first time, understanding that such actions are possible.

As the battle that rages underneath the surface continues, the benefactor knows one thing for sure. Life will never be the same from this point forward.

Saturday, May 11th
Wayne General Hospital
Wayne, NJ - 2:56PM

———————————————————

The Neurosurgeon who is handling Gary Ceepo's case has called the Neurologist into his office to discuss the matter.

Neurosurgeon: "The last scan has me worried. Instead of the swelling diminishing, it appears to be getting worse. While I know its risky, I'm afraid waiting any longer to do the surgery will place Mr. Ceepo in greater danger."

As the Neurologist studies the latest scan results, his demeanor turns from inquisitive to crestfallen: "I'm afraid you're right. Waiting until tomorrow might be a mistake. I understand that his parents flew in this morning and are here at the hospital. I think we need to have a discussion as to how to proceed."

Neurosurgeon: "I'll have the nurse reach out to them. I wish we had better options. All we can offer are two risky approaches, neither one is a guarantee that he will survive."

As the surgeon makes the call, both doctors are preparing for a discussion neither one wants to have right now.

Saturday, May 11th
Calvary Cemetery
Union, NJ - 3:02PM

_____

As Jake's team reaches the outskirts of the cemetery, they have a plan in place that offers them the best possible outcome, though nothing is guaranteed.

The FBI Regional Director, Bill Greger, has forwarded the team a photo of their prime suspect, Josef Habib.

The best picture available is a copy of his driver's license. Luckily, the person taking the picture at Motor Vehicles managed to take a snap shot that did not look like the driver was being booked at the local police station.

As both cars circle the cemetery, stopping short of the employee entrance, Kent Baldauf is already inside. He climbed the fence near the tree line, offering him the best possible cover.

The plan calls for Ava and Tricia to gain entry by flashing their badges to the security guard at the employee gate. The main office and visitor welcome center is situated close to that gate for obvious reasons.

Jake and Keri Ann will enter through the main gate, as if the only purpose for the visit is to pay respects to a friend who has passed away. They are well aware that the terrorists will be monitoring the entrance, waiting for their arrival.

As Ava and Tricia enter the rear gate by flashing the guard their credentials, they park their car in the employee parking lot, behind the welcome center/office. Things are about to get real.

Upon entering, there appears to be five people browsing the cemetery layout that is front and center on the wall. From what they can tell, it looks like two couples and a lone woman, all of which are trying to locate the gravesite of a loved one.

As Ava and Tricia approach the desk, they are greeted by a gentleman who smiles before speaking: "Can I help you?"

Ava flashes her badge while indicating that he needs to lower his voice: "We need to talk to whoever is in charge. There may be someone presently in the cemetery that is considered extremely dangerous."

The gentleman first looks around the room before speaking. He then begins to talk in a whisper: "We only have three people working today in the office so I guess I'm in charge right now."

Tricia opens her phone to Habib's picture and leans forward: "Have you seen this person today?"

The guy behind the counter looks like he's about to panic. His voice seems to have raised a full octave higher as he speaks softly, a combination that does not go together very well: "He was in here about an hour ago. He told me he wanted to find the gravesite of a friend. I never gave it a second thought?"

Tricia: "Was he alone?"

Manager: "As best I could tell. There could have been someone outside but he came in alone."

Ava: "Did he say anything else that might be important for us to know?"

Manager: "Nothing that I can recall. I told him where he needed to go and he left. I had no idea that he may be anything more than a typical weekend visitor."

Tricia, looking toward a private office in the back of the room: "Can we have a little more privacy? There are a few things we need to discuss."

As the three head to the office, Alaina Assis, who has managed to avoid detection by keeping her back to the visitors, turns slightly to observe all three entering the office and closing the door behind them.

Alaina, dialing up Habib: "We have two members of the anti-terror team on sight. They just went into a private office with one of the employees. I suspect Jake Patrick is either on premises or minutes away."

Habib: "You need to wait outside for them to leave. We have to know where they are heading."

Alaina: "Have you heard anything from our young friend since Jake Patrick left his office?"

Habib: "Nothing at all, he very well may have been compromised. Fortunately, he knows nothing of importance that might interfere with our plan."

Habib: "We have to assume that Jake Patrick and his team might be expecting an ambush, which means we need to be very careful."

Habib: "Once you know where the two team members are headed, relay their location to everyone and then proceed to your attack position. We cannot begin our assault until everyone is in place."

As Alaina ends the call, she leaves the office to prepare for her assignment.

She fails to notice that there are only two cars in the parking lot and two couples left in the office, an error in judgement that will not bode well for her.

Inside the Private Office

Tricia: "Who else is working today other than the three of you here in the office?"

As the man tries to collect his thoughts under duress, his attempt to remain calm and in control is not going well: "There are two guards on duty, each one is assigned to an entrance. You met the guard manning the employee entrance, his name is Luis. Bill Reynolds is the person assigned to the main entrance."

Ava: "Are the guards armed?"

Manager: "We do not permit any employee to carry a firearm. This is not a facility that offers a criminal anything of value."

Tricia: "What about other workers?"

Manager: "We always have four maintenance workers on duty at all times, in case we receive any complaints about conditions at some of the grave sites. When we are actually preparing sites for new arrivals, that number goes up by six, including operators of the heavy equipment necessary for digging."

Ava: "So there are four workers on premises?"

The manager nods his head in agreement but realizes that today is an exception: "I forgot that one of the workers called in sick this morning. There are only three on duty."

Tricia: "Do you have a way of communicating with everyone?"

Manager: "I can reach the guards at the entrances and I can communicate with the maintenance manager on duty via a walkie talkie. Its up to the manager to know where his workers are at all times."

Ava, changing the subject for the time being: "We need to try and get everyone else off the property before someone gets hurt. The first order of business is for you to show me where the gravesite of Michael Lemmo is located."

The manager responds to her question with a surprised look on his face: "That's the grave that the man asked me about."

As they make their way into the welcome center, there is just one couple left in the office. As the manager points out the section where the grave is located, the three of them remain as calm as possible to avoid any possible disruption.

Tricia, still whispering as they head back to the office: "We need you to send your two worker's home without letting on that anything is wrong. As for you and the guard, you need to begin searching the remaining sections of the cemetery, informing anyone in the area that they must leave the cemetery through the employee exit. Make up some story about irrigation problems that are beginning to flood out the front entrance area. Do not indicate anything that could cause panic."

Ava: "After clearing the area, both you and the guard leave the cemetery the same way."

Manager: "What about the front guard and the maintenance crew?"

Tricia: "I suggest you try to reach them. My guess is that they have already been compromised."

As the manager begins, using the walkie talkie to reach the maintenance crew, Tricia and Ava can hear everything that transpires. After three attempts to raise someone, its obvious that no one is going to answer.

Ava: "Now call the front gate, putting your phone on speaker. Don't react if someone answers that you do not know."

As the manager dials the number, after the third ring the phone is answered. The guard begins to cough as he attempts to speak: "I'm having a bit of an allergy reaction. What's up?"

The manager, following the lead provided to him: "I'm just checking in to see if everything's all right."

Guard, still coughing, in an effort to hide his identity: "No problems. Let me go so that I can get this cough under control." He them hangs up the phone.

Manager: "That's not Bill, no matter how hard he tried to cover it up."

Tricia: "Okay, we have to assume the worst. There's a cemetery car parked in the rear, can we use it?"

As he gets the keys and hands them to Ava, he looks as if he's going to pass out. His day has turned out to be memorable, but not in a good way.

Ava: "As soon as we leave, get rid of the couple outside by telling them they need to leave the cemetery through the rear exit, using the same excuse about the irrigation system. Then you need to lock the front door and try to get as many people out of the cemetery as possible. Don't go anywhere near Mr. Lemmo's gravesite."

As Tricia and Ava leave the office from the rear door, the manager is telling the only remaining couple inside that the office is closing and they need to leave the premises.

––––––––––––––––––––––––––––––––

As Alaina continues to watch the front door, she sees a cemetery vehicle leaving the area, exiting from the rear of the building.

The car is marked clearly as belonging to Calvary Cemetery. She doesn't give it a second thought until a couple leaves the office and gets into the last remaining car in the parking lot. As she begins to realize her mistake, she is left with no one to follow.

Alaina contacts Josef Habib: "I think I made a mistake. It appears that the two anti-terror team officers left from the rear in a cemetery car. I thought it was one of the workers. I have no idea where they are or how to find them."

Habib, displaying anger in his voice: "Just get back here and take your position. The plan goes ahead no matter where they are."

Habib is furious but committed to carrying out his mission to the end.

He now knows that Jake Patrick and his team are in defense mode. Whether they suspect an attack or are just being thorough matters little right now. His team cannot protect him from the rocket that will end his life.

––––––––––––––––––––––––––––––––

As Jake and Keri Ann remain outside the cemetery waiting for an update before continuing any further, his phone rings indicating that Ava Matthews is about to provide that update.

Jake: "Ava, did you learn anything helpful?"

Ava: "The terror cell is on the property and planning an assault. It appears that they have overpowered the main entrance guard and, what appears to be, the maintenance staff, which includes a manager and two grounds keepers."

Ava: "Any worker you see, near or around the gravesite, does not work here. We arranged for the office staff to leave the premises. As for the manager and the rear gate guard, they are going to approach anyone who is in the four rear quadrants, away from your location, to leave immediately through the employee exit."

Jake: "Okay, we've done all we can do to keep things under control. The both of you know what you need to do. I'll touch base with Kent and then we'll enter the cemetery."

Jake dials up Kent before proceeding: "Kent, it appears we will get the chance to end this today. We have confirmed that our terror cell is here."

Kent: "I suspected as much. No need to let things go any further."

Jake: "Where are you?"

Kent: "I'm making my way around the perimeter of the cemetery looking for anything that might be out of place. I suspect our friends will be somewhere nearer to Mike's gravesite."

Jake: "I'm told that any employees you encounter are fake, including the guard at the entrance."

Kent: "That's good to know. I'm going to try to target as many of the jihadists that I can before they see me. No reason to begin this fight blind. I'll call you later."

As the phone line goes dead, Jake looks over at Keri Ann: "Are you ready to do this?"

She nods in the affirmative as Jake starts the car and begins the journey that will end this nightmare, once and for all.

Chapter Nineteen

Getting All Your Ducks in a Row

Saturday, May 11th

Saturday, May 11th
McGinnis's Campaign Headquarters
Middletown, NJ - 3:03PM

As the weekend office staff prepare to leave for the day, Dakota Whalen enters the building, passing the staff workers by, as she makes a beeline for an unscheduled meeting with Laurie Duffy.

After receiving that unexpected phone call from Robert O'Reilly, its time to have a heart to heart discussion with her friend. If Dakota's instincts are correct, the last thing she wants to do is blindside Laurie with her upcoming article.

As Laurie is preparing to close down the office for the day, she is facing away from the door, shutting down the copier. As she turns around, she is startled to find Dakota Whalen staring back at her.

Laurie, reacting to her visitor: "You scared me half to death. If you arrived ten minutes later, you would have found a locked door. A phone call would have been better than just showing up."

233

Dakota: "I just need a few minutes of your time. Something has come up that cannot wait. There are a few questions that I need answered and you're the only person I trust who will not try to spin it in any way."

Laurie: "It sounds serious. I know we had to cancel our meeting the other day but I never thought getting together was so important to have you drive all the way down here to see me."

Dakota: "Laurie, can we sit for a minute. I promise that I will not keep you very long."

As they both take a seat, Laurie looks toward the Congressman's office before responding: "Everyone has left for the day, so if your questions require someone higher in the ranks, you are going to be disappointed."

Dakota: "I'm here to see you, not them."

Laurie: "Okay, what's on your mind?"

As Dakota prepares to address her concerns, she begins searching for the right words that will keep Laurie from taking a defensive posture. After all, Laurie has worked for the Congressman for quite some time. Her loyalty must run deep.

Dakota: "I had a troublesome phone call this morning that has me concerned. What can you tell me about Robert O'Reilly?"

Laurie: "Why, did Bob call you?"

Dakota: "Before I get into any of that, just give me a thumbnail sketch of the man. I promise to fill you in before we're done."

Laurie: "Bob was instrumental in getting Dan elected to Congress. He was hired as a media expert to help plan his first campaign. It went so well that Dan began depending on Bob to clear a path through the mind field that is politics."

Laurie: "They became friends along the way and Dan relies on him a great deal, which is how Bob became his Chief of Staff. He's pretty much in charge of this campaign, which just took a significant bounce after the attacks, as I'm sure you are aware."

Dakota: "I find political campaigns to be less about the issues and more about the candidate. Only in politics can an attempted assassination result in voters changing their allegiances. How could the attacks make him a more qualified candidate?"

Laurie: "Welcome to my world."

Dakota: "Do you like Bob, personally?"

Laurie: "He's okay, I guess. He's a little too intense for my liking but he gets results. Everything Bob does has an agenda attached to it. If it's not going to help with the campaign, he has no interest. He's what you would call a **ONE TRICK PONY**."

Dakota: "O'Reilly called me earlier and wanted me to lie to my readers in return for an exclusive interview."

Laurie, looking astonished by what she just heard: "He did what?"

Dakota: "He asked me to pretend that I had talked to a number of voters that might have been on the fence but moved into Dan's camp because of the attacks. They were so angered by the attacks that they found themselves supporting Dan because of his bravery under fire and that their support of Dan was a way of thumbing their noses at the attacker."

Laurie, looking amused for the first time: "I'm sure you told him where he could shove his interview?"

Dakota: "I've said nothing about the request as of yet. His shameless assumption had me thinking that the attacks might not have been initiated by someone looking to get to Dan. What if O'Reilly orchestrated the attacks to earn the sympathy vote? Dan has been languishing behind for months now. If he stayed there much longer, chances are he might never catch up to Trooien."

Laurie, finding Dakota's remarks to be unthinkable: "There's no way Dan would ever go for that. Deep down, he's a boy scout. I work with him every day and know him better than you do. He was genuinely shaken to his core by the attacks. He feels lucky to be alive."

Dakota: "What if Bob arranged for the attacks without consulting Dan? The shooter missed him at the rally, even though every expert I could find felt that the shot, taken in an open field, was not a difficult one."

Dakota: "As for the bombing, Dan's car never got close enough to the blast to put him in any danger. The truck driver, who's vehicle broke down, is a little too convenient for my liking."

Laurie: "You're way out of line with this theory of yours. Both attacks were not without ramifications."

Laurie: "Dan's security guard could have been killed. There were dozens of people hurt and killed by the blast. None of that chaos and tragedy would be considered acceptable collateral damage for a political campaign. That would make Bob nothing more than a monster."

Dakota: "Politics can be a dangerous game. Many people have crashed and burned as a result of political actions taken by an opponent. While this one was a little more visceral, there's nothing that suggests that hurting bystanders was a part of the plan, just a by-product."

Dakota: "Maybe the shooter was ordered to miss? Maybe the bomber was supposed to ignite the blast from a safer position? When playing such a dangerous game, things happen. You can't control everything."

Laurie: "I can't believe this is happening. Do you really believe that Bob organized these attacks?"

Dakota: "I'm not sure what I believe just yet. All I know is that O'Reilly, during a scary time for Dan McGinnis, thought it a good idea to try and capitalize on the incidents to increase the chances of his candidate winning the election. That, at the very least, is a problematic thing to do, don't you think?"

Laurie: "I'm not sure what it is you want me to say?"

Dakota: "I'm just looking for whatever insight you can give me on the man. I have nothing concrete that suggests he had anything to do with the attacks. If not for that phone call, none of this would have entered my mind."

Dakota: "Do you think he's capable of arranging the attacks in order to help his candidate?"

Laurie: "I'm not sure what I believe. Bob is certainly intense, which is why he's so good at his job. Could he go so far as to place people in danger just to gain favor with the voters? I'm finding it hard to believe he would ever risk his and Dan's careers for a few more votes."

Laurie: "The one thing I can say for sure is that Dan would never approve of such a thing. If Bob chose to defy conventional ethics, he did so on his own."

Saturday, May 11th
Senator Trooien's Residence
Bedminster, NJ - 3:05PM

Liz Anderson has spent the last few hours trying to motivate the captains of each precinct to keep their people in a positive state of mind during the hiatus.

Every hour their people remain on the sidelines feels like a day lost. When running a campaign, every second counts. Lost momentum has a way of turning into lost opportunities.

Liz: "With every passing hour, we are losing ground. I can barely find Phil's name being spoken anywhere. Dan McGinnis, even though he remains silent, is still dominating the coverage. This has to end soon or there will be nothing left to salvage."

Howard Clarke: "I have to agree with Liz, Phil. The only candidate being shut out is you."

Phil Trooien: "We are going to have to tough it out for the time being."

Meanwhile, Roberta Trooien is sitting in the corner of the room, remaining quiet as Phil and his team lament the circumstances that have led to this day.

Roberta decides she can't remain quiet any longer: "This is so unfair. Because of some madman, Phil is forced to remain silent while his opponent receives all the press. The citizens of New

Jersey are being manipulated into supporting a candidate that has no business running to unseat Phil in the first place. He has little going for him except for his charisma and his desire to use it to his advantage."

Roberta: "Phil is the only person capable of helping the citizens of the state. He's dedicated his life to them and this is how they show their appreciation?"

Phil, Howie and Liz sit in silence as Roberta allows her feelings to permeate the room. They understand that she is coming from a different place. She loves her husband and sees this whole mess as a personal attack.

Phil: "We all agree that we have been dealt a bad hand, Roberta. What we need to remember is that we still have six months before the election. In politics, where opinions can sway significantly in a stiff wind, all of this can go away before anyone fills out a ballot."

Liz Anderson, trying to be careful not to dismiss Roberta's emotional outreach: "Roberta, we all feel the same way but we need to look ahead, not back. Phil's right, there's plenty of time left to turn this around."

Howard Clarke:"No one is less patient than me. If there was a way to begin countering the recent polls today, you can bet I would be the first one on it. No one has ever unseated a United States Senator that has a track record as good as Phil's. McGinnis will not be the first to do so."

Phil: "Okay, we need a plan that we can implement the minute the pause is lifted. Let's put our energy into that rather than playing the **WHAT IF** game."

As everyone settles in for a strategy session, the entire team hopes that Jake Patrick can end this nightmare quickly. Their political livelihoods rest in the balance.

Saturday, May 11th
Calvary Cemetery
Union, NJ - 3:16PM

_____

As Jake and Keri Ann pull up to the gate, they are aware that their arrival will be monitored carefully. They must suppress their natural instincts and pretend to be oblivious to their surroundings. They are just here to pay their respects to a fallen comrade who gave his life in the line of duty.

As they reach the guard shed, a middle eastern man in a uniform, comes out of the shed with a map: "If you give me the name or the location number of the gravesite you are visiting, I can guide you in the proper direction."

Jake: "That won't be necessary. We have been to the site on numerous occasions and we know where we need to go, but thank you."

Guard: "Not a problem. Please be aware that the cemetery closes today at five."

Jake: "We will be gone long before that, I can assure you."

As they enter the cemetery, driving slowly and with purpose, Jake turns to Keri Ann as he connects the intercom that links his entire team to one another: "Our store owner Abdul Farouk has a second job. He's pretending to be the guard at the entrance."

Ava, over the coms: "They must think he's unrecognizable. His only contact was at the bombing and he was well hidden from view."

Jake: "We need to get eyes on him as soon as possible. When the action starts, I do not expect him to remain at the front gate."

Ava: "Tricia and I will patrol the area. Driving a cemetery vehicle should provide enough cover to avoid any suspicion. When we get closer to the entrance, I'll find an isolated spot that gives me a view of the guardhouse. Tricia can continue without me."

Jake: "Although the cemetery looks to be empty Tricia, you need to take a quick survey of the grounds surrounding Mike's grave to make sure that we do not have any innocents in the way. Anyone too close to the action needs to leave as quickly as possible."

Making his way around the exterior limits of the cemetery, Kent is using the scope on his rifle to survey the area for potential targets. The property nearer the fence is heavily wooded, providing him excellent cover.

As he gets closer to the mausoleums with their above ground tombs, he notices something moving in his peripheral vision. As he focuses in, he sees a man hiding behind the farthest structure, carrying a rifle.

Kent, over the coms: "I've found our truck driver, Mohammed Sarif. He is waiting in the wings to ambush the two of you. He has no idea that I'm in range to ruin his day. Do you want me to take him out before he can try anything?"

Jake: "Not until we have a better handle on their plan of attack. I doubt they plan to engage us in a gun fight. That would not end well for them. Until we can locate the rest of their team, especially the leader, we need to pretend that nothing is out of the ordinary."

Ava: "Are you still opposed to bringing in law enforcement as a backup?"

Jake: "We have to do this ourselves. If we try and cover our backs and the bad guys get wind of it, they might cancel their plans and head for the hills. All that will do is allow them the chance to set up another ambush, one that we may not have advanced warning of, which could prove deadly."

As Jake and Keri Ann pull up to Mike's gravesite, they prepare to leave the car and begin the final stages of their plan.

Each is wearing the necessary body armor under their clothes and both have a hidden firearm, in case anyone gets too close for comfort. Their link to the coms and the rest of their team will be the only protection they have from any unseen danger.

As Ava and Tricia drive closer to the front entrance, Ava sees a position behind the tree line that should offer her enough protection. She grabs her rifle and exits the car while they are hidden from view of the guardhouse.

From this point forward, Ava's assignment is to neutralize Abdul Farouk before he can do any damage.

As Tricia continues to circumnavigate the property, she notices two maintenance workers fairly close to Jake and Keri Ann's position. They appear to be preparing a new gravesite, using shovels: "Jake, there are two workers located at nine o'clock, apparently digging a new grave."

Jake: "It looks like our terror cell is larger than we thought. Could one of them be Alaina Assis?"

Tricia: "I'm afraid not, Jake. It's two men who want us to think they are just doing their job. I suspect they are armed."

As Jake surveils his surroundings, he can see them through the tree line: "I have them in my sights. They will have to be our responsibility. We need the rest of you to find Josef Habib and Alaina Assis. Until we do, this remains a crap shoot."

Tricia: "I'll leave these two in your capable hands."

Tricia continues driving, heading toward the mausoleum section from the opposite side of the cemetery from Kent. It appears to be one of the only locations that offer significant cover. As she makes her way closer, she can see a car parked about 200 yards from the maintenance building: "There's a car over here that looks familiar. I'm sure I saw it parked at the office."

Ava, over coms: "Is there anyone in the vicinity that might be visiting one of the graves? There were two couples in the office, along with a single woman, when we arrived. It could be one of their vehicles?"

Tricia: "The surrounding area is pretty open. If they are visiting a grave, they parked in the wrong area. I'm going to pull up to the car and check it out."

Jake: "Tricia, please approach the car carefully."

As Tricia pulls up behind the car, she holds her handgun by her side, exiting the vehicle. Choosing to approach the car from the passenger side, she crouches down, hiding from view of the windows. As she reaches for the door handle to open it, she finds it unlocked.

She quickly swings the door open calling out to anyone inside: "I need everyone inside the car to please exit the vehicle carefully. I'm an officer of the law. The last thing I want to do is hurt anyone."

As nothing but silence fills the air, Tricia decides to back up slightly and try the rear passenger side door before exposing herself to anyone inside. As she reaches for the handle and tries the door, it swings open as well, revealing the car to be empty.

Tricia, allowing her heightened emotions to subside: "There's no one in the car."

Jake: "If the car was in the parking lot at the office, someone who was inside could have been part of the terror cell."

All of a sudden Tricia gets an epiphany: "The woman inside by herself could have been Alaina Assis. We never saw her face, just the back of her head."

Jake: "Then they know that we are here in force. The surprise factor is off the table. We need to act quickly."

Jake, talking over the coms to everyone: "Let's make sure we are all on the same page. We are aware of six terrorists with loyalty to Josef Habib. One is back in Morristown while two are pretending to be working on a gravesite close to me and Keri Ann. That leaves our four remaining jihadists, Farouk, Sarif, Assis and Habib."

Kent: "There are no guarantees that we have accounted for everyone. With such a high degree of uncertainty, things could get out of hand."

Keri Ann, speaking to the team for the first time: "Sometimes you need to trust your instincts, especially when time is not on your side."

Keri Ann: "Mine keeps telling me that this is a four person terror cell. They have already committed three major attacks, neither of which required more assailants than those that we have identified."

Keri Ann: "I suspect that Habib was our sniper, since we found no one else on any of the surveillance videos. While he appears to be in his sixties, I doubt any of us were looking for an older jihadist among the crowd on the camera feeds."

Keri Ann: "We learned about our store owner Farouk from a local Iman. When we found him at the scene of the car bombing, he was already on our radar."

Keri Ann: "We identified Alaina Assis from the traffic cams as being the lookout when Gary was attacked. As for Mohammed Sarif, using one of his company vans during the rocket attacked placed him front and center on our suspect list."

Keri Ann: "My instincts tell me that Josef Habib fired the rocket. Being the one in charge, he wanted to be the person to kill Jake. Having suffered a loss of pride when his target never showed that day, I have to believe that Habib is the person who will attempt to provide the lethal blow today."

Keri Ann: "In short, we can't waste time looking for additional terrorists when there is no time to waste. We have Farouk and Sarif in our sights. I have no doubt that Josef Habib and Alaina Assis are nearby."

Keri Ann: "Finding them before we have to engage would give us a greater chance for success while minimizing the possibility of injury. Our number one priority right now has to be finding them."

As Keri Ann finishes her diatribe, the silence over the coms is deafening. Jake decides to speak: "Does anyone have a different opinion?"

As the coms remain silent, Jake takes charge of the situation: "Tricia, you need to find Assis and do it quickly. No matter how we do it, we are going to need some luck to find Habib in time before he can act."

Jake: "Kent, you're the best field agent we have on the team. We need you to eliminate Sarif when I give the order and then its up to you to locate Habib before he can launch his attack. I doubt he's using a sniper rifle or any close combat weapon of choice. I suspect he's hiding somewhere close, waiting for his opportunity. How many hiding places can be out here in the open?"

As Jake is talking, Tricia Highland speaks over the coms: "I've got her. She's on the roof of the maintenance building, not too far from the mausoleums. She's trying to remain hidden from view but she will have to raise herself up before she can take a shot. She appears to be carrying a rifle."

Jake: "Can you take her out?"

Tricia: "I'm positioned behind a tree near the building. She will not get a shot off before she's out of the fight."

Jake: "Okay, that gets us closer to ending this on a positive note. Here's how we plan on proceeding."

Chapter Twenty

Just One Spark Can Start a Fire

Saturday, May 11ᵗʰ
Somewhere in New Jersey - 3:18PM

As the benefactor stares on the clock, the word coward is front and center. No call was made, no admissions were revealed and no warning was issued.

I never thought that I was capable of ignoring the right thing to do, especially when it could lead to the death of another human being. I'm not the person I thought I was.

I have always prided myself on my compassion for others. I guess rhetorical empathy is a lot easier when there is nothing significant on the line?

Placing my life and my reputation above all else has cost another human being his life. The shame I feel at this moment will never go away.

For the first time I can understand how someone may be willing to end their life. With no way out, and seeing

little value to your existence, no plan that would end the
suffering would be off the table.

Saturday, May 11th
Calvary Cemetery
Union, NJ - 3:27PM

———————————————

Kent Baldauf has always taken responsibility for his actions. At this moment, he's placing the safety of his entire team on his shoulders. They have one more terrorist to find and it's his job to find him.

Today, years removed from his overseas operations, he hopes that his luck will hold out, at least until the end of the day.

His team maintains the rest of the terror cell in their sights, except for the primary player, Josef Habib. Not only is he the key to all of this, he remains the chief assassin, while every other member of his terror cell is window dressing. Habib expects them to be the distraction that will allow him to finish the job.

Kent closes his eyes and begins to allow himself to go back in time to when his senses and reflexes were the difference between life and death.

Every patrol in enemy territory could end in tragedy for himself and his squad. Failure to locate the enemy in time placed everyone unprotected, not the best place to be in a war zone.

Where could he be hiding? It has to be someplace close
enough for him to accomplish his mission. This is primarily
an open area with few places to hide. Its time for me to
rely on muscle memory, both physically and mentally. He's
close by, I'm sure of it.

As Kent begins to use the scope on his rifle as if it was a makeshift pair of binoculars, he begins surveilling the entire perimeter, searching the tree line and ending with the maintenance building.

He can see, for the first time, Alaina Assis peeking up from the rooftop and he can also see Tricia Highland, well positioned to take her out. As he scans closer to the main entrance, he can see Abdul Farouk moving in their direction and away from the gate. He can also see Ava Matthews following him from behind, ready to end him as a threat when the fighting begins.

From Kent's vantage point, the entire battlefield lies in front of him.

Knowing the skillset of his team and their ability to react quickly and lethally, none of these radicals should pose a problem when the action begins. Can they distract our team long enough for Habib to react?

I've got to find him. It's the only way to be sure we all stay alive.

If he's inside the maintenance building, he will need to exit before attacking, as there is no clear trajectory open to him. He must know that his people will not last long once the shooting begins. That might be a risky move on his part.

If he's inside one of the mausoleums, which seems unlikely, he may be able to react quickly but he may not know where Jake is at the moment he exits. That delay alone might be too problematic for him.

Where else can he be? His hiding place should be obvious.
The answer is staring me in the face. Why can't I see it?

––––––––––––––––––––––––––––––––

The time for confrontation has arrived.

Jake tells everyone over the coms that he's going to neutralize the terrorists pretending to be digging a new grave. He knows that once he does so, chances are the status quo will end.

Jake: "The quicker we neutralize the rest of the terror cell the better. Since we have yet to find Habib, we cannot allow ourselves to remain distracted for any length of time."

Tricia: "Do you want me to try to make it to the roof? From my present vantage point, she has to rise in order for me to act."

Jake: "There's not enough time for you to do so. Just take her out the moment she provides you with a target."

Tricia: "Directive understood."

Ava: "I can take out Farouk now if you want. Just say the word."

Jake: "If he does not pose a threat, wait until you have no choice but to act. He may be in contact with Habib. The less warning Habib has the better."

Ava: "I understand. If anything changes, I will use my best judgment, but he will not be a threat to us, that I can assure you."

Kent: "I'm still looking for Habib but Mohammed Sarif is an easy takedown. Just say the word."

Jake: "My advice is the same. Once I neutralize the two foot soldiers, all bets are off. If anything changes, I trust all of you to do what you think is right."

———————————————————

As Jake prepares to act, he looks at Keri Ann before moving toward the workers: "This will not take long. Once it starts, I'll need you to duck behind the tombstone. You can't give any of the remaining jihadists an easy target."

Keri Ann: "Why are we not approaching them together? If we each take one out, there's less chance of something going wrong?"

Jake: "The only way I can approach them without it appearing to be a threat is for you to stay here. The two of us would never reach them before they realized something was up. I have to go alone."

Keri Ann: "Just make it back to me."

———————————————————

As Kent sees Jake heading toward the jihadists, he decides he needs to trust his own instincts.

He places the silencer on the business end of his rifle and quickly puts Mohammed Sarif in his sight, pulling the trigger before he has any idea that his life is about to end.

As Mohammed falls lifeless to the ground, Kent positions himself in Jake's direction and lines up his next potential targets, the two groundskeepers.

———————————————————

As Jake approaches, he calls out to them, pretending that he needs their assistance: "Excuse me guys, can you help me with something?"

The terrorists appear to be nervous and agitated but unsure of what they need to do.

The younger of the two jihadists drops into the hole that has been dug recently, dragging his rifle with him, which was hidden under a cloth. Confronting their prey was not in the plan.

Before Jake can reach their position, the two jihadists begin to separate themselves further apart, as the one above ground moves away from the gravesite. Jake can sense that things are getting more complicated.

Before Jake can get any closer, the radical quickens his pace. Jake responds: "Where are you going? I just have a simple question to ask. It's not complicated."

Ignoring Jake's words, the confusion on their faces turn to rage. The one above ground reaches into his waistband. A pistol comes into view as he points it in Jake's direction.

Unfortunately for him, Jake's reflexes are better as he takes him down with one shot to the head.

In the split second it takes to neutralize his fellow radical, the one in the newly dug grave has his rifle pointed in Jake's direction. Before he can fire, Kent blows a new hole in his head, just above his eyes, throwing him back against the dirt wall, as his rifle flies skyward.

As Jake sees the rifle in his peripheral vision, he hears the whistling sound of Kent's bullet, a sound he is quite familiar with from his time overseas. As he turns to address the second

252

terrorist, he sees him falling backward, ironically landing in an empty gravesite.

Jake, over the coms: "To whom do I owe my life?"

Kent: "Once they moved apart, the odds were no longer in your favor. All I did was take back the advantage."

Kent: "I still have not found Habib. No need to remain hidden. I'm heading toward the maintenance building, it's the only cover I can see that might provide him with a place to hide."

———————————————

As soon as the shooting started, Abdul Farouk began running in the direction of Jake and Keri Ann.

Ava Matthews was right behind him but his back was to her. She has never fired upon anyone that was not an immediate threat to her well being and she wasn't going to start now.

As he begins to narrow the gap between himself and Jake, Ava decides to end this chase now: "Abdul, stop running, there's no place for you to go."

As Abdul reacts to the sound of her voice, he turns to face Ava with his rifle pointing at the ground. The shocked expression on his face gradually turns to anger: "Allah has blessed this day, a day that will see the end of Jake Patrick. Nothing you can do will keep us from honoring Allah on the battlefield."

Ava: "Your fight is over so just place the gun on the ground."

Ava can see him fighting a personal battle with himself. Should he give up and be humiliated in the eyes of Allah or ignore the fear that is consuming him and prepare to reap his rewards in the afterlife?

As she carefully watches his facial expressions, she can see which side he has chosen. Abdul drops the rifle at his feet and begins to raise his hands in the air, but only as a distraction. Without warning, he reached behind his back and pulls out a handgun, raising it towards her.

It will do him no good as Ava brings him down with a shot to the heart. As he lays there in silence, she can't help but wonder if the afterlife he's looking forward to reaching was worth the journey? No matter, her conscious is clear. She still has not killed anyone who was not a threat to her or to someone else.

From the moment Jake initiated the confrontation, Tricia Highland has remained focused behind her scope with the rifle pointing at the roof above. As she hears the first shots ring out, she tenses for what is to come.

Within seconds, Alaina Assis rises from her position, pointing her rifle in Jake's direction. She does not notice the danger that it just yards below her. As she appears to be mumbling some prayer, she raises the rifle to a firing position, only to be thrown forcibly to the ground as Tricia fires from below.

Immediately, Assis is neutralized as her rifle flies into the air and her body disappears from view.

All Tricia can do is hope that her teammates have successfully done their jobs as well. As for their primary concern, the whereabouts of Josef Habib, there's been no talk over the coms to suggest he is not still in play.

That leaves Jake in a precarious position. Whatever plan Habib has to end Jake's life, he remains a threat. No one is safe until everyone is neutralized. It looks as if the worst possible scenario in now the only one left, Habib can still accomplish his mission.

The team may have to be a split second faster while remaining in the dark. When he shows himself, they have to be better and faster than he is.

As Jake begins running back to Keri Ann's position, the calls come over the coms telling him that Alaina Assis, Mohammed Sarif and Abdul Farouk are no longer a threat. That leaves their leader, Josef Habib as the only remaining terrorist.

As he makes it back to Keri Ann, they both drop to the ground behind Micheal's gravestone. They are protected from view, assuming the maintenance building and the mausoleums are the most likely hiding place for Habib.

Jake, over the coms: "Tricia, Habib has to be somewhere near you. Be very careful but you need to begin canvassing the area."

Ava: "Jake, I'm heading in that direction as well. I'm coming in from the other side of Kent's location, so we can cover more ground."

Josef Habib is sweating profusely. He's beginning to panic. There's nothing about the weather conditions to cause such a reaction in him. His nerves are at a breaking point as the time to act grows near.

Why hasn't he received any updates? From his vantage point, he cannot see anyone nor should he. His only chance of success is to remain completely hidden from view until the exact moment arrives for him to act.

He's lying low in the rear of an opened top maintenance truck with the rocket launcher at his side, loaded and ready to fire. In order to hide from view, he's placed a canvas tarp over himself, supported by a number of crates that give the appearance of normalcy to the truck.

He can see in Jake's direction, which is how he arranged the truck, but unfortunately, he's not high enough to observe Jake's movements or the movements of his fellow jihadists. Once the firing began, he was supposed to be getting updates from his team as to what is taking place and when he needs to launch the rocket.

With the firing happening in all directions and no updates coming his way, he has to assume that his team is falling one by one before they can do any damage. That leaves him on his own.

He clutches the rocket launcher tightly in his hands and prepares to jump from the truck. All he can hope for is that Jake Patrick is still somewhere in front of him, giving him a target to aim toward.

My life will end today but it will not be in vain. I must complete my mission and bring honor to BAHRUN by taking Jake Patrick into the afterlife with me.

Allah, please give me the strength to complete my task in your honor. If you can provide me one last blessing, let me look into the face of this most vile infidel as I send him into oblivion.

As Habib tenses his muscles and prepares to rise from his prone position, all hell breaks loose as the truck explodes in a ball of fire, sending it high in the air and throwing Habib from the rear onto the ground, still clutching the launcher.

Josef Habib is both confused and in a great deal of pain as his world begins to collapse around him. While there appears to be blood surrounding him, most likely his, he tries to regain his senses before attempting to complete his mission.

He has one chance to regain control. As he tries to get a grip on the rocket launcher, his ability to stand is more difficult than he had anticipated.

As Habib begins searching for his target, there's someone standing close by, making no attempt to move in his direction. His vision is still cloudy from the blast and all he can see are shadows.

As he tries to focus on the man, he sees a rifle pointing in his direction. Could this be Jake Patrick? He tries to lift the rocket launcher but it feels like it weighs hundreds of pounds as he's losing blood faster than he can possibly imagine.

Kent Baldauf just smiles in his direction before speaking: "I know we just met but I'm afraid it will be a brief encounter."

Kent then pulls the trigger, hitting Habib in the head and throwing him to the ground as the rocket launcher lands safely by his side. Kent then picks it up and disengages the rocket, insuring that there will be no accidents.

Kent, over the coms: "I know I waited to the last minute to find him, but better late than never, or so the saying goes. Habib is now with his virgins, if his religious beliefs are worth anything."

As silence settles in for the first time since the shooting began, Jake and his team meet up near Michael Lemmo's resting place as they hear the sirens in the distance.

I guess the neighbors surrounding the cemetery must have thought the **END OF DAYS** was near as the quiet cemetery was coming to life and not in a good way.

They have a lot of explaining to do to the authorities but the threat is over and every member of the team is still standing, except for Gary Ceepo, who is fighting for his life because of the actions of Josef Habib.

Jake, turning to Kent: "How did you find him?"

Kent: "Actually, I acted on pure instinct. After having exhausted all possible hiding places, I noticed a small open backed truck near the maintenance building. It didn't appear threatening nor did it seem possible for anyone to be hiding in such a small space, but it was the only possible hiding place left."

Kent: "Before heading inside the maintenance building, which was a last ditch effort on my part, I decided to roll a grenade under the axle to see what happens. I guess I got lucky."

As the team begins to relax, they all smile in his direction, knowing that Kent was just being Kent.

Keri Ann, being a professional profiler, responds to Kent: "I'd love to have a chance to dig deep into your psyche. You seemed to be wired differently than everyone else."

Kent, turning to Jake: "Is your wife flirting with me?"

Jake: "Keri Ann, that's a journey you may regret taking."

As they gather their thoughts, Jake addresses the team: "The rest of the day will be used to recharge our batteries and relax after today's ordeal."

Jake: "As for me, I'll relax after getting an update on Gary's condition. We missed having him here today."

Jake: "Before closing out the case, we need to complete the final piece of the puzzle by exposing the political operative that put all of this into motion."

Jake: "However, all of that can wait until tomorrow. I want everyone to take the rest of the day off."

Saturday, May 11th
Jake and Keri Ann's Residence
Morristown, NJ - 6:47PM

After leaving multiple messages on Gary's father's phone, he has yet to get a call back. All that has done is raise Jake's anxiety level. Waiting around has never been something he was comfortable doing.

Jake: "I'm going to go to the hospital. There's no way I can relax without an update on Gary's condition. Something tells me things are not going well."

Keri Ann: "I understand how you feel but your calls are not their top priority right now. The last thing they may want to do is talk on the phone."

Jake: "You may be right but I have to do something. What I know for sure is that everyone is quick to spread good news, bad news not so much. I can't help but think his condition falls into the latter."

As if on cue, Jake's phone rings, indicating the call is coming from Gary's dad. He looks at Keri Ann and then answers the call with the phone on speaker: "I've been hoping you would call. Gary's entire team is worried about him."

Gary's dad: "I'm sorry it took so long for me to get back to you. Gary has had a setback, leaving the doctor's with limited options. They had hoped the swelling would subside enough to allow the surgeon to operate. Unfortunately, the opposite has happened."

Jake: "If they can't operate, what can they do?"

Gary's dad: "That's just it, he's in the operating room right now."

Gary's dad: "The swelling could only be alleviated via surgery. It's far riskier but they were left with no other viable option. We expect him to be in the operating room for hours. Hopefully, they can reduce the swelling and still have enough time to repair the damage. He can only stay under anesthesia for a limited amount of time."

Gary's dad: "I wish I had better news for you. Unfortunately, there are no guarantees. All we can do is pray."

Jake: "I'm sorry to have bothered you. You can be assured that all of our prayers are being sent Gary's way right now. We have no problem coming to the hospital to provide moral support for you and your wife, if it might help?"

Gary's dad: "That's kind of you but we prefer to be alone right now. I promise to call you when we learn anything of importance."

Jake: "Okay, but please remember that we are just a phone call away."

As Jake ends the call, he's having difficulty controlling his emotions. He's experiencing a sense of dread that is far worse than anything he had to endure at the cemetery.

Jake's team has lost members over the years but this would be harder to deal with knowing that Gary should never have been in that car.

As for now, all Jake can do is pray and ask God for one more favor, to spare the life of his good friend.

Chapter Twenty-One

Picking Up the Pieces

Sunday, May 12th
Office of the NJ Special Projects Task Force
Morristown, NJ - 7:14AM

Jake received a call from the hospital around **6:00AM**. The call came from the Administrator's office at Wayne General. He was told by the hospital employee that there was a request for him to come to the hospital at his earliest convenience.

The woman calling had no information about Gary's condition or the reason she was asked to make the call, just that she was following orders.

All Jake could think about was how bad news tends to be cloaked in secrecy. It's always the news you do not want to hear that makes itself known in whispers.

Jake felt the need to go to the hospital in mass, so he reached out to the rest of his team to meet him at the office. Whatever they were about to encounter, they needed to do so together.

Ava: "I can't believe that the person contacting you knew nothing of Gary's condition."

Tricia: "We may be overthinking this. Hospitals are not the most thoughtful of institutions. They deal with all levels of emotions on a daily basis, trying to remain objective in the process. I, for one, choose to avoid assumptions."

Kent: "Let's get this over with. We can't change anything so I suggest we get over there and learn what there is to know. Whatever it is, we deal with it as a team."

As they leave for the hospital, everyone is well aware that the New Jersey Special Projects Task Force might look differently at day's end. None of their skills nor their experience can alter this outcome.

Sunday, May 12th
Somewhere in New Jersey - 7:20AM
_____

The benefactor was unable to sleep a wink.

The evening news reported about the chaos that occurred in Calvary Cemetery yesterday afternoon, which resulted in the death of a number of people, all suspected of being radical jihadists.

There were no details, other than the fact that they confronted a formidable force, who took them down without any innocent civilians injured in the process.

The press had no names of anyone involved in the melee (may-lay). Though unusual, it's not uncommon when dealing with terrorism. This could have been one small part of a larger and more dangerous terror cell.

While the press may still be in the dark as to the details, the benefactor knows all too well what went down.

Jake Patrick must have nine lives. The skill level of his anti-terror team is well documented, but taking down an enemy that had the element of surprise in their favor is no small task.

Where do I go from here? I doubt this whole mess will end just because the bad guys are no longer among the living. The information we were given was confidential. Someone must have told them that Jake was going to be at the cemetery?

I'm relieved to know that Jake survived the attack. I never wanted anyone to die. This was all a mistake. I let my emotions get the best of me and I thought I could tip the scales in our favor without anyone getting hurt or being the wiser.

I guess its true that letting emotions dictate one's actions is the same as having a fool for a client. Whether in a court of law or in the pubic domain, the truth will eventually rule the day. As for now, we will just have to see where the cards begin to fall next.

Sunday, May 12th
Wayne General Hospital
Wayne, NJ - 7:52AM

————————————————

As Jake's team enters the waiting area, anyone who does not understand what they are going through might find their reactions to be odd, if not downright unusual.

On one hand, they are anxious about Gary's condition. On the other hand, they cannot help but be fearful of what might be coming their way.

The result is four people whose expressions suggests the need for an immediate answer while their movements suggests otherwise, as if the longer it takes to reach the desk, the less chance they will hear bad news.

When finally making it to the desk, Jake is the first to talk: "My name is Jake Patrick. We were asked to come to the hospital for an update on the condition of our friend, Gary Ceepo. Can you point us in the right direction?"

As the person behind the desk hits a few buttons on her computer, she shows a look of understanding on her face as she responds: "It looks like they are waiting for you in Room 218 on the second floor. The elevator is down the hall to your right."

Ava: "Does it say anything else on your screen that we need to know?"

Receptionist: "It just says for me to direct you to the right room. I'm sure things will be a lot clearer upstairs."

As they head to the elevator, everyone remains silent. Speculation is over.

As the elevator opens on the second floor, they can see that room 218 is down the corridor on the left. As they make their way to the door, all four look at the handle as if it is electrically charged, waiting to jolt whoever dares to touch it.

As Jake takes charge and opens the door, he finds Gary's parents and what appears to be one of the doctors, hovering over the bed. They all turn at once with smiles on their faces.

The only voice they hear is Gary saying: "It's about time you got here. I thought you forgot about me?"

Gary's lying in the bed with a number of monitors attached to multiple parts of his body. They can see he's still groggy and not fully awake but the atmosphere in the room says all they need to know, Gary will be okay.

Gary's dad: "He made it through surgery with flying colors. They were able to reduce the swelling, revealing the need to have a couple of internal bleeds repaired before they could close him up. They feel they got all of his issues addressed. The rest involves a long period of recovery."

Surgeon: "We got lucky is about all I can say. It may take him a month or two to get back on his feet, but barring any further complications, he should make a complete recovery."

As they all gather around him, he falls back to sleep. It appears he has been coming in and out of consciousness for the past few hours. They happen to arrive during one of his more cogent moments, allowing them a chance to hear him interact before dozing off again.

Gary's dad: "It's going to take a few days before we can expect to have him awake for any length of time but that's a small price to pay to have him back with us."

Surgeon: "We need to keep him under most of the time. When dealing with the brain, the unconscious state is a lot better for the healing process than having him awake and alert."

The relief on the faces of Jake and his team could light up a room. Its as if they won the Super Bowl. Once again, God was on their side. The team is well aware that such divine guidance can be finite, but for today, its alive and well.

Sunday, May 12th
A Very Important Meeting - 10:18AM

_____

Jake's phone call to arrange this meeting was more of a demand than a request. The sense of urgency expressed by Jake required immediate compliance, creating a high level of anxiety for the campaign team.

As Jake arrives for the meeting, he's not alone. He's accompanied by the rest of his team members.

As they enter the office of Senator Phil Trooien, he's sitting at his desk with his Chief of Staff, Howard Clarke, and his campaign aide, Liz Anderson in attendance, as requested.

As the four sit down, Phil is the first to talk: "According to the papers, I understand there was an altercation yesterday afternoon in Union, NJ?"

Kent: "I guess an altercation is one way you can describe it? Being ambushed by a terror cell might be a little more serious than an altercation but why quibble over semantics."

Phil: "Because we were aware that you were going to be in the cemetery yesterday, are you suggesting that we somehow let that information slip out, resulting in the ambush?"

Phil: "I can assure you that no one here did anything of the sort. If someone put you in danger, it did not come from us. Why would we break your trust?"

Howard Clarke: "Why would either campaign do such a thing? Your team was trying to get to the bottom of this mess. Ending this nightmare would be best for both parties. We both could get back to campaigning, which is all we wanted to do."

Liz Andersen showing her level of confusion: "I'm not sure what is going on right now. You told us that the attacks had a terrorist connection, not a political one. Based on what we read this morning, it appears that your conclusion was correct, assuming the bodies found at the scene were indeed radical extremists. Why are you here?"

Jake: "I'm afraid we lied to you about this being terror related rather than politically motivated. While there was a terror cell involved, they were acting on behalf of a political agenda, at least in the beginning, one that we believe was initiated by someone in this room."

Phil, showing his annoyance over this entire matter: "This is absurd. Why would anyone here be dealing with terrorists? What possible motive could we have to do such a thing? Besides, we were told that both campaigns were privy to the information concerning your whereabouts yesterday. Why do you think it had to be one of us?"

Tricia: "Once again, I'm afraid you were lied to about our motives. Once we determined that this whole mess was initiated by someone either in your camp or Congressman McGinnis's, we set a plan in motion to limit the suspects further."

Jake: "We intentionally told both campaigns different stories. While your camp was told about the trip to the cemetery, McGinnis's team was given an entirely different location for my whereabouts. Obviously, the terrorists were directed to the cemetery, placing the leak from inside this room. One of you, or all of you, are in a great deal of trouble."

As Phil Trooien, Howard Clarke and Liz Anderson appear stunned by this latest revelation, the looks on their faces suggest a level of innocence that is hard for Jake to ignore.

Jake has profiled hundreds of people over the years and he has become proficient at noticing even the slightest **TELL** that would give away the true intentions of a suspect.

He sees nothing on the faces of the three to indicate they are trying to deceive him in any way.

Jake: "I must say that the three of you are managing to keep me guessing as to who may be the person responsible. Whoever you are, the best way to avoid having your life turned upside down and having the book thrown at you would be to fess up to your involvement."

Jake: "I can assure you that I will not rest until every stone is unturned, every detail of your life has been examined and every chance you may have had for some degree of leniency will have vanished."

As the three remain in shock, unable to respond, a voice comes out of the corner of the room: "I'm the one you are looking for."

As everyone turns, Roberta Trooien is standing in the doorway with tears running down her face: "None of this was supposed to happen. No one was to get hurt. All I wanted to do was scare Dan McGinnis into dropping out of the race."

As everyone sits in shock, Phil rises from his seat and approaches Roberta, letting her fall into his arms as the tears

269

turn to sobs and her legs begin to falter. Phil grabs her tightly to keep her from falling.

As Liz runs to get her a chair, Phil places her down, remaining by her side: "What in God's name were you thinking? None of this makes any sense. How did you manage to keep this from me? When the casualties started adding up, how did you not tell me what you did so that I could help put a stop to this madness?"

Roberta, trying to calm her nerves enough to allow herself to speak: "I was so angry when Dan decided to run against you. He was your friend. You helped him on numerous occasions when he first got into politics. How could he do this to you?"

Roberta: "After all the good things you have done for the citizens of New Jersey, to be betrayed for your kindness with lies, innuendoes and inferences that suggested you failed the state during your tenure, it was more than I could stand."

Jake: "Why did you let things escalate after the security guard was shot in Toms River? That should have been enough for you to shut it down."

Roberta: "I was livid about the shooting. He was ordered to miss, not to hit anyone. When I confronted him, he assured me that it was the best way to make my point. A miss would never scare him enough to withdraw. The shooter told me he would never kill anyone. If I wanted Dan out of the campaign, this was a necessary first step."

Phil: "I can't believe I'm hearing this? How could I not know what you were planning?"

Jake: "What about the bombing?"

Roberta: "He said that would be the final straw. He would arrange to allow Dan to get close but never to be in danger. I never had any idea he would detonate the bomb in such a manner as to kill and maim innocent bystanders?"

Roberta: "After the bombing, I tried to shut it down but I was no longer in control. He threatened me with exposure if I did not help him get to you. It appears he was using me all along."

Before continuing, Roberta felt the need to clarify something: "I don't want you to think I was afraid for myself as much as I was afraid for Phil. If I thought I could admit to my mistakes without crushing his campaign, I would have done so. New Jersey needs him to be their Senator. I could not allow anyone to destroy my husband and the good he's done for the state."

Jake: "What led to yesterday?"

Roberta: "I knew, based on my conversations, that he would destroy Phil's career, if not worse. He only pretended to cooperate in order to find a way to get closer to you, Jake."

Roberta: "From that moment on, his threats grew significantly, including physical harm, if I did not find a way to lead him to you. When we learned of your plans, I was in too deep to back off."

Roberta, beginning to cry once again: "I thought about calling you a few times before your trip to the cemetery but I didn't have the courage to do so. In the end, the coward in me won out. I will forever live with that failure."

Roberta, turning to Phil: "I'm so sorry, Phil. I've succeeded in hurting the one person I wanted to protect."

This day would end the way Jake intended but with a culprit no one expected.

David P. McMullan

Politics can be a cruel master. When one accrues a level of power that separates them from the masses, it can be so addictive that losing it is a fate worse than death, even for those that just exist in its afterglow.

Roberta Trooien not only wrecked her own life, she destroyed others around her, the unexpected consequences of her actions.

For the first time, Jake was exposed to real power. To his surprise, he was beginning to realize that fighting terrorism was safer than trying to understand the world of politics, in which every person looking to grab the brass ring are willing to do just about anything to achieve their objective.

Politics is a game that few can play without abandoning their principles. Those that refuse to play usually end up on the wrong side of power, a side that offers little chance for success.

As for Jake, hopefully he can avoid any contact with politics in the future. They play too rough for his liking.

He prefers terrorists, who wear their hatred on their sleeves, not hidden behind rhetoric that camouflages their real intentions.

Chapter Twenty-Two

And So It Goes

Wednesday, May 29th
Office of the NJ Special Projects Task Force
Morristown, NJ - 9:27AM

A little over two weeks removed from the assault at the cemetery, Jake Patrick is completing his report to the Governor, summarizing the five days that followed the shooting in Toms River, NJ.

There were a number of surprises that turned heads, overshadowing those that played out as expected.

As Jake was compartmentalizing his thoughts for the report, his team had already placed this latest chapter in their rear view mirror, something Jake always had difficulty doing, probably because he's responsible for everyone else.

At the top of his report was the good news story of how Gary Ceepo survived the attack and was making a miraculous recovery. He is expected to be released from the hospital this upcoming weekend, although he still will have months of physical therapy ahead of him.

273

After coming so close to death, the trials that still await Gary are numerous but manageable. He's a survivor and no matter how long it takes, Gary's team will patiently wait for him to return to duty.

As Jake's report turns its focus on the political landscape, things did not end well for Senator Trooien and his re-election campaign. With his wife, Roberta, pleading guilty for the role she played in the attacks on Congressman McGinnis, Senator Trooien's political career was left in shambles.

Just a few days ago he announced that he would not be seeking re-election in November.

Jake felt terrible about Phil's political demise. He was a friend and, by all accounts, he knew nothing of what Roberta had done, leaving him to take the brunt of the criticism.

A good man that did a lot for New Jersey will forever be stained by the scandal that rocked the state, leaving him a legacy of shame, something he does not deserve. Roberta's attempt at saving his legacy wound up destroying it instead.

As for Congressman McGinnis, one would think he would benefit from the scandal surrounding his opponent, but you would be mistaken.

After Dakota Whalen printed her story about his Chief of Staff's attempt to capitalize on the attacks, he could not distance himself from Robert O'Reilly. The public outcry forced him to abandon his campaign for the Senate seat.

With less than six months remaining before election day, it's anyone's guess who might find themselves to be the new Senator for the state of New Jersey come inauguration day.

Jake had less sympathy for Dan McGinnis than he had for Phil Trooien. By all accounts, Dan approved of Bob O'Reilly's attempt to sway the press, making him a willing participant, not an enviable position for a politician to find himself when fighting for votes.

As for the terror angle, with the elimination of the latest terror cell on American soil, the word on the street suggests that BAHRUN is pretending they acted without authorization, a claim that borders on the absurd.

No terror cell would activate on their own. By pretending otherwise, BAHRUN is finding themselves losing face with other radical extremists. Rather than enhancing their status, they are heading toward insignificance, a fate worse than death.

Jake suspects a battle brewing within the ranks. Those responsible for this fiasco could very well be heading for an early grave. It's always good news when terror organizations begin fighting among themselves. We all benefit when they turn their attention elsewhere.

Finally, Jake found yesterday's front page article in the New Jersey Herald to be quite enlightening. Dakota Whalen, one of the state's most highly regarded investigative journalist, did a take on politics that mirrored his own views on the subject.

Jake never considered himself to be a political junky. While he had his opinions and voted regularly, he chose candidates that, on the surface, appeared to be in sync with his beliefs.

While reading the article, Jake found it comforting to learn that he was not alone when it came to politics. There are others who refuse to allow it to consume their lives, Dakota Whalen being one of them.

When terrorism and politics collided on his watch, he had no choice but to enter both worlds. Being forced to interact, he learned more about politics than he cared to know.

It appears, based on her article, that Dakota Whalen has similar concerns.

Jake found her article short but to the point. It was so profound that he decided to add it to his report. She expressed what many citizens feel about their elected officials and the oath they take in order to serve.

As for Jake, hopefully, his journey into politics was one and done. It's way too disturbing a place for him to dwell within.

Dakota Whalen's Front Page Article on Politics

Many of you know me as an investigative reporter, a person that unabashedly will turn over every rock in order to provide you with the truth about crime and those that have chosen to break the law to further their own needs and desires.

I have never been much of a political person, though I do love our country and feel blessed to have been born here.

As best as I can tell, the freedoms we cherish are not the norm but the exception, something we should never forget or risk losing due to neglect. Once lost, they will be difficult to resurrect from the ashes that will be left behind.

Our Founding Fathers left us with a document that has managed to survive for nearly 250 years, though at times in our history, it's survival was far from a guarantee.

Recent events have shown a bright light on politics as my investigative world, which deals mostly with crime, managed to collide with the political landscape.

What I learned about politics along the way has opened my eyes to another danger, one that hides itself behind a blanket of respectability and prestige.

Politicians desperately try to keep the masses at bay, away from the underlying truth that the people's representatives have another master, far more powerful and more influential, that demands the bulk of their time and energy, leaving the needs of the people a distant second.

What I'm referring to is the desire for power. One can easily get addicted without being aware of its web. While it is not as debilitating as other addictions, it can lead to one's demise just the same, taking many of us along for the ride.

I'm sure that most politicians enter the landscape with good intentions. Their desire to serve may have been their initial intent but once they enter the inner sanctum, few can avoid it's alluring scent.

We are all dependent in some way on those that we elect to office, hoping they will be our voice and our champion when the need to do so arises. When the lure of power turns their heads, moving them further away from their constituents, we are among the last to know.

There's only one answer, in my opinion, that could remove the temptation once and for all. What we need to do is establish term limits on every one of our representatives. If they know their time in office is limited, their need to maintain what is finite by nature, would appear less intoxicating.

Maybe they would remember their oath to serve someone other than themselves?

Until that day comes, politicians will constantly be running for office, using whatever means necessary to win the next election and maintain their hold on power.

Sadly, without term limits, their constituents will remain nothing more than an afterthought.

———————————————————

As Jake finishes his report, he shuts down his computer and heads to the conference room, directing his team to follow him for a much needed strategy meeting. He can finally put this case aside.

As for his team, they have no illusions that the calm of today is fleeting and fragile.

There's always someone else that places their radical ideas above all else and chooses to blame America and its freedoms for the ills of the world. When they, once again, decide to show their head, Jake's team will be ready.

The End